第一代美国华裔文学和朝裔文学比较研究

郭冬辉　刘振前　著

北京交通大学出版社
·北京·

内 容 简 介

本书以第一代华裔美国移民作家的作品为关照，以第一代朝裔美国作家的作品为参照进行对比分析，时间跨度以两个亚裔美国种族文学开始为起点，以1965年为阶段终点。第一代华裔和朝裔美国作家从各自的视角书写了东方主义原型人物与真正东方人物的差异。华裔美国作家展现了文本角度的多重性，而朝裔美国作家则表现出强烈的民族特性。这些移民作家书写了出亚裔种族文学的类别性、多重性和不均衡性，挑战了种族书写的文化霸权，表达了不断进化的亚美经历。

图书在版编目（CIP）数据

第一代美国华裔文学和朝裔文学比较研究：英文 / 郭冬辉，刘振前著. —北京：北京交通大学出版社，2023.10

ISBN 978-7-5121-4346-3

Ⅰ. ① 第… Ⅱ. ① 郭… ② 刘… Ⅲ. ① 华人文学–文学研究–美国–英文 ② 朝鲜人–文学研究–美国–英文 Ⅳ. ① I712.06

中国版本图书馆 CIP 数据核字（2022）第 036823 号

第一代美国华裔文学和朝裔文学比较研究

DI-YI DAI MEIGUO HUAYI WENXUE HE CHAOYI WENXUE BIJIAO YANJIU

责任编辑：张利军

出版发行：北京交通大学出版社　　电话：010-51686414　　http://www.bjtup.com.cn

地　　址：北京市海淀区高梁桥斜街44号　　邮编：100044

印 刷 者：北京虎彩文化传播有限公司

经　　销：全国新华书店

开　　本：170 mm×240 mm　　印张：10.125　　字数：190千字

版 印 次：2023年10月第1版　　2023年10月第1次印刷

定　　价：49.00元

本书如有质量问题，请向北京交通大学出版社质监组反映。

投诉电话：010-51686043，51686008；E-mail：press@bjtu.edu.cn。

Preface

This book concentrates on Chinese American literature by the first-generation immigrant writers, making some comparisons with that by Korean American writers, with the time span extending from the different beginnings of two Asian American ethnic groups to 1965 as its termination. As nascent literature, Chinese and Korean American writers articulate the double-voiced discourses from different perspectives to display the absolute difference between stereotyped characters in Orientalism and the real oriental image through writing about an almost-forgotten past.

The twofold voices of multiplicity and nationalism articulated by the main part of Chinese and Korean American writers echo each other and manifest the prime features in the two branches of Asian American ethnic groups. The majority of first-generation Chinese immigrant writers manifest multiplicity: ambassadors of goodwill, nostalgia, reminiscence, complaints, acculturation, the cultural transformation, protest against racial discrimination and appeal for acceptance and tolerance in the new land, Americanization and assimilability, presenting a more picturesque version of the Chinese immigrants in a covert and oblique way on the one hand. Within the early Korean American literature by most first-generation Korean American writers, the bulk of them display strong Nationalism of resistance in oppositional terms to Japanese occupation or Western imperial culture, epitomizing Korea and the Korean patriotic spirit in their literature instead of Korean Americans in the U.S. on the other hand. They expose a collective trauma, the displacement from the ancestral homeland with yet an attachment to the home in term of custom, language and folk culture that exist consciously or subconsciously in the memory.

Meanwhile, there are two distinctive figures that remain unique among their peers because both of them do not follow the routine line but offer alternative voices on the immigrant life in the host land against the strategies adopted by most Chinese and Korean American writers. Sui Sin Far's *Mrs. Spring Fragrance*, without intention of appealing to the curiosity of the American reading public, deconstructs the thinking mode of exclusive discrimination based on racial binary oppositions, ethnocentrism and scientific racialism by subverting the state-sanctioned racial stereotyped Other and exposing racial discrimination jeopardy so as to reconstruct a utopian world where people of all races live harmoniously with the idea of universality of human nature as its core and one family as its form. Younghill Kang interrogates the life on the new land and manages to deconstruct Emersonian American dream by keeping the contradictions between the promise of freedom and the reality of race discrimination, between economic survival and dreams of intellectual accomplishment, and between the ideal of America and actual experience of life in its margins existence, and simultaneously subvert Franklinian American dream with his four major Korean immigrants who fail to achieve their American ambitions respectively in *East Goes West*.

It is clear that these cultural warriors of the first-generation immigrant writers articulate different voices and manifest the variety, diversity, and indeed the unevenness of the literature, to the everlasting benefit of our future generations. The double-voiced discourses in the works of the majority and the unique of the Chinese and Korean American groups build bridges that span generations and nationalities between men and women, connecting Asian Americans to each other, to other minority groups, to American society and beyond. The hegemony of racist writing about Asians and Asian Americans is, to some extent, being challenged each time

Chinese and Korean American voices emerge in an effort to define and express the unique and ever-evolving Asian American experience.

Here we wish to earnestly express my heartfelt gratitude to the following scholars and friends whose direction and help we forever cherish. The finished work has benefited from so many people's contributions although there is only a single name on it.

To start, my gratitude goes to Professor Liu Zhenqian, my co-author, under whose intelligent, patient and enlightening guidance this book is finally completed. His profound knowledge and preciseness in the academic scholarship makes this book far better than it would have been.

My hearty thanks go to Professor Hyunsook Kim, my supervisor. She has been a talented mentor, a skillful trainer, a benevolent mother and an inspiring cheerleader with combined rigor and compassion which have made me a lot better than I would have been. Once and again she makes the worst good and the best better for me, which offers me new hope and courage to hold on straight to the end. Her benevolence and nobility in the moral quality have set an eternal example for me to follow in the rest of my life no matter where I am.

I acknowledge my gratitude to Professor Yootaeck Sohn, Professor Yongkwan Lee, and Professor Youngran Koh, whose lectures and seminars have broadened my horizon in literature. Their instruction and humanity broaden my vision and enrich my thoughts. I also acknowledge my gratitude to Professor Mi-jae Lee, Professor Kyong-hark Kim, and Professor Hang-jin Yoon who give me inspiration and thoughtful suggestion which benefit me enormously during my study.

Last but not least, I want to thank my family, who give me their love, tolerance, and support freely, and from whom, during all these long years of my study, I have escaped the duties of being a filial daughter, a nice wife and a patient mother. They understand me and give me unceasing encouragement and forgiveness. I am especially grateful to my father who supported me in every possible way in every stage of my life. Without the love and support from my family, it would be impossible to finalize this book.

With the help of such unselfish individuals, this book has been strengthened, and I alone am responsible for the flaws and misinterpretations.

Thank you all from the bottom of my heart.

The author
2023-10

Contents

Chapter 1

Introduction

This book examines Chinese American literature by the first-generation immigrant writers by 1965, making some comparisons with that of Korean American literature. As nascent literatures, Chinese and Korean American writings by the first-generation immigrant writers have received scant attention. Thus, this book aims to focus on the double-voiced discourses uttered by majority of Chinese and Korean American writers on the one hand, and two unique figures who, different from their contemporaries, offer alternative voices on the immigrant life in the host land on the other hand. Thus, this book unfolds itself along two main lines. The first line is a proposition which holds general voices articulated by the bulk of Chinese and Korean American writings of the first-generation immigrant writers. Their double-voiced discourses echo each other and manifest the main features in the two branches of Asian American ethnic groups. The second main line of the book is to integrate two unique figures in Chinese and Korean American literatures — Sui Sin Far and Younghill Kang who, apart from the pack of their contemporaries in the literary circles, articulate different voices against the strategies adopted by most Chinese and Korean American writers to deconstruct and challenge the accepted state-sanctioned thinking modes.[①]

With the development of pluralism and the efforts of Asian American ethnic groups, literary works created by Asian American writers attract more and more attention. The once ignored marginal field is burgeoning, and has much to tell the world about Asian American literature as a body of work, as a subject of inquiry, as a node and as a window onto transnational realities. However, Lisa Lowe detected the internal diversity and distinction under the umbrella term of Asian Americans in her *Heterogeneity, Hybridity, Multiplicity: Asian American Difference* published in the spring of 1991:

> "From the perspective of the majority culture, Asian Americans may very well be constructed as different from, and other than, Euro-Americans. But from the perspectives of Asian Americans, we are perhaps even more different, more diverse, among ourselves: being men and women at different distances and generations from our "original" Asian cultures — cultures as different as Chinese, Japanese, Korean, Filipino, Indian, and Vietnamese — Asian Americans are born in the United States and born in Asia; of exclusively Asian parents and of mixed race; urban and rural; refugee and non-refugee... fluent in English and non-English speaking; educated and working class. As with other diasporas in the United States, the Asian immigrant collectivity is unstable and changeable, with its cohesion complicated by intergenerationality, by various degrees of identification and

① By the word of "to deconstruct", I mean to negate, undermine, subvert, counterattack and break the accepted thinking mode.

relation to "homeland," and by different extents of assimilation to and distinction from "majority culture" in the United States." (Lowe, 1991)[27]

Just as Lisa Lowe discerns the noticeable heterogeneity, hybridity and multiplicity in the field of Asian Americans, the intra-ethnic diversities, differences and similarities exist in the territory of Asian American literature.

Correlating with Lowe's heterogeneous, hybrid and multiple differences within the umbrella term of Asian American, I notice that literatures by Chinese Americans and Korean Americans share the same points in the difference because of the diverse factors of socio-history, demographical changes, Eastern tradition and culture, etc. Three reasons prompt me to focus on Chinese and Korean American literatures under the umbrella of Asian American literature. First, the comparative issue of Chinese American literature and Korean American literature is a field worth going into because it could make Chinese and Koreans discern our own countries objectively. Although the highly diverse individual voices of Chinese American writers and Korean American writers are reducible to no single measure, their recurrent voices reflect psychological and cultural dilemmas specific to Chinese Americans and Korean Americans.

The other reason is that the United States of America gave special attention to Japan, but neglected China and even considered Koreans as Japanese after Japan occupied Korea in 1905. For the most of general American public, the term of Asian Americans mainly refers to people of Chinese and Japanese origins, even if more people are immigrating from Korea. Since Euro-centric American minds ignore the diverse cultures and nations of Asia, the world's largest and most populous continent, there is a critical value to discover similarities and differences among different literatures by marginalized Chinese American group and Korean American group because Chinese American literature and Korean American literature are not alien, but they represent their world, reflecting their images and voices.

The last reason is that both Chinese Americans and Korean Americans share the similar and miserable immigrant history besides holding the same race of Mongoloid, inheriting the similar cultural background, deriving from the very same land, and being ignored by the U.S. When they came from Asia across the Pacific rather than from Europe across the Atlantic, Chinese immigrants and Korean immigrants found they were not allowed to feel at home in the United States, and even their grandchildren and great-grandchildren still find they are not regarded and accepted as Americans in some ways. Both of Chinese and Korean Americans are regarded as others not simply because of their lack of indigenous ties to American society after their migration to a foreign land, but also because of their specific receptions. First of all, they had natural qualities they could not change or hide — the shape and color of their eyes, the color of their hair, and the complexion of their skin, etc. Next, unlike European immigrants who were able to blend into the society of their adopted country by changing their names or by shedding their past, their ethnicity — the language, customs, dress and culture of the old country because they are physically indistinguishable from the whites in America, Chinese and Korean immigrants could not transform themselves felicitously for they brought Asian cultures rather than the traditions and ideas originating in the Greco-Roman world. Then, the class interests of white capital as well as white labor forced Chinese and Korean immigrants as others because the immigrants came to meet demands for labor — plantation workers, railroad workers, miners, factory operatives, cannery workers and farm laborers, etc. Pushed out of competition for employment by racial discrimination and white working class's hostility, most of Chinese and Korean immigrants had to shift to be shopkeepers, merchants, and small businessmen. Self-employment was the only way of survival which was a response to racial discrimination and exclusion in the labor market. At last, unlike European immigrants, Chinese and Korean immigrants were also victimized by the institutionalized racial discrimination of public policies. *The Chinese Exclusion Act* of 1882 singled out the Chinese on a racial basis and *the National Origins Act* of 1924 barred the entry of women from both China and Korea. The laws determined both who could come to the United States and who could become citizens as *the Naturalization Law* of 1790 had specified that naturalized citizenship was to be reserved for whites and remained in effect until 1952. Since citizenship is a prerequisite for suffrage — political power essential for groups to defend and advance their rights and interests, Asian immigrants, unlike their European counterparts, were not permitted to exercise power and were prohibited by the laws of many states from land ownership. *The 1922 Cable Act* went even further, providing that any American woman who married an alien ineligible to citizenship shall not be a citizen of the United States.

Thus, Chinese and Korean immigrants of the first generation confronted with the similar institutionalized racial discrimination in their trans-Pacific odyssey, in which like those immigrants from Europe, the immigrants from Northeast Asia regarded America as an ideal place for a fresh start, sought to build a new life in the brave new world and became one part of the American dream. Yet, both Chinese and Korean immigrants did not permit exterior demands to determine wholly the direction and quality of their lives, manipulating their life they had thought beyond their capabilities and emerging from the state of an invisible minority in the United

States, although they confronted so many challenges from the reality of discrimination and the natives' reactions that they were pushed to a kind of geographical and cultural margin where old norms became detached.

Chinese and Korean American literatures are based on the similar experiences which have been mentioned above. Meanwhile, the two branches of Asian American literature display heterogeneity and multiplicity. Both Chinese and Korean immigrants came from Northeast Asia, a small homogeneous village which is peopled with heterogeneity. Even though Chinese and Korean American literature had been regarded the same in the category of Asian American literature due to sharing so much similarity in experiencing the ignorance and racial discrimination from the American mainstream society and Northeast Asian origin, Chinese and Korean American literatures possesses differences in that the two essentially different ethnic groups of immigrants were unconsciously influenced by diverse cultures and historical vicissitudes and thus harbored implicit cultural separatism.

Chinese and Korean American literatures by the first-generation immigrant writers by 1965 will be focused on. Referred to here as the phase of Asian estrangement, it describes a century of racial exclusion and cultural deprivation legitimized through institutionalized socio-economic and political practices. The post-1965 phase, as the period characterized by an apparent legal inclusion of Asian Americans, witnessed a dramatic change in the population, legal status, socio-economic security, and general presence of Asian Americans in American society. The time span of the first-generation immigrant writers in Chinese and Korean American literature extends from the different beginnings of two Asian American ethnic groups to 1965, with its termination being marked by the passage of *the 1965 Immigration and Nationality Act* which finally abolished the annual Asian immigration quotas. If Asian American immigration by 1965 reflected a history of economic exploitation and socio-political oppression exemplifying the institutionalized structural racism as foregrounded by the internal colonial model, this racism adopts a different guise in the post-1965 phase.

On the other hand, as the foundation of the later boom and prosperity in Asian American ethnic literature, the various perspectives of Chinese American and Korean American writings by the first-generation immigrant writers are the genesis of the present eminence as a main current in American literature. In principle, works in the initial stage of Chinese and Korean American literatures declare the starting of the Chinese immigrants' and Korean immigrants' entrance into American literature thereby, spiritually enlightening, profoundly influencing, and paving the way for the new generation of Chinese and Korean American writers. The bumper harvests and the inevitable progress by the younger generation derive from, in no small measure, to the great contribution made by the first generation of writers in the initial stage. It is very natural that the children of Chinese and Korean immigrants are able to penetrate deeper into the mainstream American culture with the foundations laid by all the ancestors' efforts. Since these predecessor writers have made much greater contribution to Asian American literature, it is worthwhile to study further on the first generation of Chinese and Korean American authors and their writings in the initial stage.

The critical reviews on Chinese American literature have effectively advanced the exploration of the texts created by the Asian Americans with Chinese ancestry, broadened people's vision, and deepened their understanding of the writings. However, up to now, in China, texts written by Korean American writers are beneath the attention of literary critics who scantly scrutinize the comparative study between

Chinese American literature and Korean American literature. Almost none of these critics from either Chinese or Korean perspectives distinguish the self-expression of the early stage of the writings from another. Nor do they help us see development of an ethnic literature that bears resemblance to other ethnic literature in the United States because ethnic literature is often regarded as a form of regional literature with limited meaning, relevant only to the individual communities and irrelevant to the mainstream society.

The study of Chinese American literature is a new development in the field of American literature both at home and abroad. Despite the fact that Chinese American literature has existed in the United States for more than one hundred and fifty years, the body of writing has been ignored by most American critics until 1960s, since it was considered to lack aesthetic value. Moreover, cultural barriers have also hindered the recognition of Asian American literature. However, with the increasing size of the Asian American population, its growing significance in American society and culture, and the expanded appreciation, both popular and academic, of Asian American literary works — all these progresses have converged to stir wide interest in scholarly work on topics related to Asian American literature. Ever since the publication of Elaine H. Kim's *Asian American Literature: An Introduction to the Writings and Their Social Context* in 1982, myriads of articles, books, and researches have appeared in the field of Asian American literary studies. Chinese American literature has always occupied a major position in these works and Korean American literature has developed rapidly with each passing day. It seems evident that both Chinese American literature and Korean American literature are beginning to find their places in Asian American literature, a new breed of multi-ethnic American literature.

The early critical analysis on Asian American literature starts from Elaine H. Kim in the U.S. In the early stage, the few existing studies underscored the sociological and historical background of the relevant works while offering general summaries of individual texts. In *Asian American Literature: An Introduction to the Writings and Their Social Context*, Elaine H. Kim attempts to "trace the topography and rich textures of the Asian American experience as it is expressed in Asian American literature from the late 19th century to the present day" and focuses on "the evolution of Asian American consciousness and self-image as expressed in the literature" (Kim, 2006)[iii]. It is this book that made the little known Asian American literature squeeze into the American literary consciousness, and demonstrated that the body of work was large and vital enough to deserve serious scholarly attention.

With the ending of the Cold War in the early 1990s and setting in motion of another wave of global migration, multiculturalism became a popular topic among Asian American scholars. Asian American literature is seen as the less trodden path that might lead to a critical re-engagement with America. Amy Ling's *Between Worlds: Women Writers of Chinese Ancestry* (1990) is a contextual study with a feminist effort at recovering a women's literary history. Han Suyin's comment in the foreword of the book is quite to the point, when she says, "It is a breakthrough not only in the sphere of Western studies on the manifold aspects of China, but also a beacon light for Chinese historians" and "Amy Ling's book gives us that family of woman warriors — such a felicitous word, coined by Maxine Hong Kingston — a family to which, I found to my surprise, I too belong by the skin of my teeth" (Ling, 1990)[X].

Then a row of Asian American critical texts follows. All were published in 1992 or 1993, and their proximity signaled to me, potently, that a critical discourse was materializing. Then follow some best authorial studies which include *Amy Tan: A Critical Companion* (1998) by E. D. Huntle, *Conversations with Maxine Hong Kingston* (1998) edited by Paul Skenazy and Tera Martin, and *Critical Essays on Maxine Hong Kingston* (1998) by Laura E. Skandera Trombley. In the same year of 1998, Ma Shengmei published *Immigrant Subjectivities in Asian American and Asian Diaspora Literatures,* which offers a new way of reading Asian American and Asian Diaspora literatures, thereby addressing an overlapping lacuna in ethnic, postcolonial, and area studies: the construction of immigrant subjectivities.

Further studies of Asian American literature have not concentrated on the artistic elements of literary works. Sau-ling Cynthia Wong and Yin Xiaohuang have provided two authoritative accounts of the history and scope of Chinese American literature. In Sau-ling Cynthia Wong's essay *Chinese American Literature* collected in *An Interethnic Companion to Asian American Literature* (1997), her survey of Chinese American works reveals "the dialectical relationship between particular works and the social climates in which they are written" (Cheung, 1997)[21]. Another book that offers a comprehensive history of Chinese American literature is Yin Xiaohuang's sociohistorical study of *Chinese American Literature since the 1850s* published in 2000. Using a fresh approach that combines literary and historical knowledge, Mr. Yin Xiaohuang traces the origins and development of the extensive and largely neglected body of literature written in English and in Chinese from the 1850s to the present. Nowadays, plenty of researches on Chinese American literature have appeared in various journals in the U.S. Dozens of papers on Chinese American literature can be found in American journals such as *Criticism, American Literary History, Genders, Framework, Signs,* and *MELUS — Multi-Ethnic Literature of the United States*. However, these researches either give brief introduction to Chinese

American literature or focus on specific author or individual work like Maxine Hong Kingston or Amy Tan. They seldom pay close attention to works by the first generation of Chinese Americans.

Chinese American literature has drawn the attention of more and more Chinese scholars and critics. It was introduced into Chinese academia in the 1980s, when two introductory papers about Maxine Hong Kingston's *The Woman Warrior* were published and a few texts listed in syllabi for English majors in predominant universities like Beijing Foreign Studies University. In the 1990s when the course of Chinese American literature appeared in both graduate and undergraduate English curricula, some universities set up centers for Chinese American literary study that substantially improved both the teaching and literary critics in this field.[①] However, there were no noticeable follow-ups until the year of the new millennium, right after China obtained membership to the WTO, at which point a decade-long boom of academic essays and monographs on almost every Chinese American author we know of began.[②] In recent years, more and more Chinese scholars have turned their focus on the study of Chinese American literature because Asian American literature is considered to offer a critical lens for Chinese society to reflect on their own traditional cultural remaking. Owing to the efforts of Professor Wu Bing in Beijing Foreign Studies University and Professor Zhang Ziqing in Nanjing University, the

---

① Zhao Jianping from Yunnan Minzu University presented a brief overview of teaching Asian American literature in China in "Forum: On Teaching Asian American Literature Outside the U.S." of the MELUS Conference in San Jose, California, in 2012.

② Li Guicang and Xu Tingting from Zhejiang Normal University concluded a decade-long boom of academic interests in the field of Chinese American literature since China obtained membership to the WTO on November 11, 2001 in "Forum: On Teaching Asian American Literature Outside the U.S." of the MELUS Conference in San Jose, California, in 2012.

Chinese American Literature Research Center of Beijing Foreign Studies University, the foremost center for Chinese American research in China, was established in 2003. These professors have laid a solid foundation for the sustained research and teaching of this body of work. Numerous of articles could be found in various journals in China, either giving brief introductions to Chinese American literature or making studies on specific authors or texts.

For a long period of time, the study of Asian American literature in China has been limited to East Asian American literature, particularly Chinese American literature. The themes of generational gap, cultural clashes, acculturation and assimilation, cultural and ethnic identity, gender, race and diaspora always occupy a central place in the minds of scholars and students. Recently, the database of China National Knowledge Infrastructure records titles of 158 excellent MA theses and 34 PhD dissertations on Asian American literature in the past decade, with the overwhelming majority of titles on Chinese American literature. Chinese American literary study becomes a burgeoning academic field in China.

To sum up, the above critical reviews on Chinese American literature have efficaciously promoted the exploration of the texts created by the Chinese American ethnic group and intensified their understanding of the writings. However, texts written by Korean American writers are less concerned by Chinese literary critics who focus more on the writings by Asian Americans with Chinese ancestry and scantly examine writings by other Asian American ethnic groups without Chinese ancestry, let alone the comparative study between Chinese American literature and Korean American literature. Thus, none of these Chinese critics from either Chinese or Korean perspectives distinguish the self-expression of the early stage of the writings from another.

Due to the occasion that misinterpreting Asian American literature is not uncommon, Elaine H. Kim first attempts to integrate the Asian American literary voices in one book-length study of *Asian American Literature: An Introduction to the Writings and Their Social Context* (1982). Since then, the research on Korean diaspora literature has gradually become the subject of growing interest in academic circles in Korea though the position of Asian American studies in Korea still remains rather precarious. As a matter of fact, relatively few Korean Americans published their works written in English until the 1980s.

In the U.S. since 1970, some Asian American literary criticism and history has been published, prominently by Bruce Iwasaki's *Introduction: Asian American Literature*. Several anthologies of Asian American literature contain introductory essays of a general nature. However, "reviews of Asian American literature by Anglo American writers reveal that the criteria used to judge the literary merit of Asian American writing have not always been literary" (Kim, 2006)[vii]. Since some critics' familiarity with the sociohistorical context of Asian American literature cannot be assumed as it can in the case of Anglo-American literature, misinterpreting Asian American literature is not uncommon. On this occasion, Elaine H. Kim's *Asian American Literature: An Introduction to the Writings and Their Social Context* (1982) is the first attempt to integrate the Asian American literary voices in one book-length study. As a fellow Korean American, she includes Korean American literature, which is hardly more plentiful than Vietnamese American writing at the moment, and two representative Korean American writers: Younghill Kang and Kichung Kim.

While not much has been written about Korean American cultural production, many texts treated Korean American literature from a historical, sociological or psychological point of view. However, fifteen years after *Asian American Literature: An Introduction to the Writings and Their Social Context*, in her essay *Korean American Literature* collected in *An Interethnic Companion to Asian American Literature* (1997), Elaine H. Kim presents writings by Koreans in the U.S. as an ever-dynamic corpus, resistant to racism in American society, sexism in the Korean American community, and classism within a seemingly monolithic group.

In Korea, Asian American literature quickly became a popular topic among Korean scholars as the Cold War came to an end in the early 1990s. They develop an interest in studying the literature and start treating them as a critical subfield that had been neglected by mainstream scholarships in both American literature and Asian studies. It seems that Korean scholars in Korea generally accept Korean American literature as an obvious and natural part of Korean literature. Some scholars hold that Korean American novels depict the Korean immigrants' struggle with the identity crises arising from the clash of their Korean culture with western culture. Kyngpyo Hong of Catholic University notes that "Korean American writing reflects the struggle of these writers to preserve Korean identity" by tracing general themes of Korean American writing beginning with Younghill Kang (Hong, 2002)[1]. Professor Schongt'aek of Kory University argues a similar opinion in his introduction to the book *A Study of Korean Writers Living Abroad* that "literature by Korean immigrants reflects the conflict between race and nationality, and is colored with sensibilities particular to Korean culture" by arguing Korean American novels, such as Chang-rae Lee's *Native Speaker* (Hong, 2002)[8]. In the eyes of some Korean scholars, Korean American writers use English as a tool to express ideas that are, in the end, Korean, thus taking advantage of the transformative power of language. Critic Yu Snmo notes in his book *Understanding the Literature of Minorities in America* that the abundance of Korean words and "Koreanness" are meant to inform the audience about Korea (Hong, 2002)[15].

The hot issues in Asian American literature crucially matter in contemporary Korea in the new century. Korean readers have become increasingly interested in Korean American writers since 2003, the centennial anniversary of Korean immigration to the U.S. *Korean Literature: Its Classical Heritage and Modern Breakthroughs* (2003) edited by Korean National Commission for UNESCO consists of twenty-four articles that are considered valuable in the field as academic articles or critical essays that have appeared in the *Korea Journal* over the past 40 years. The present volume is comprised of 5 major sections. However, only the final section approaches Korean literature from an international perspective in analyzing the literature of Korean immigrants living abroad. The anthology is insufficient to promote the understanding of Korean American works although it could serve those who seek a comprehensive understanding of Korean society and culture.

A brief look at the critical writing about Korean American literature in Korea shows that scholars agree on three points. First, Korean American literature has an educational and didactic value because it informs non-Korean readers about Korea by applying Korean words and phrases in the English texts. Second, Korean American literature demonstrates and performs Koreanness hence preserving Korea culture for future generations to come. Third, Korean American literature is seen as a part of Korean literature because it discusses issues relevant to Korean culture.

To sum up, most of the literary critics from the three places of the U.S., China and Korea focus on Asian American ethnic literature, Chinese American literature by Asian American writers with only Chinese ancestry, Korean American literature by Asian American writers with only Korean ancestry, from the individual perspective of Americans, Chinese and Koreans, respectively. Almost none of these critics from either Chinese or Korean perspectives distinguish the self-expression of the early stage of the writings from another. Nor do they help us see development of an ethnic literature that bears resemblance to other ethnic literature in the United States because ethnic literature is often regarded as a form of regional literature with limited meaning, relevant only to the individual communities.

The characteristics of the Chinese American literature manifest multiplicity in that the Chinese American writers tend to delve into the broad issues of ethnic identity, cultural conflicts, sentiments of the native-born and immigration experiences, etc. Different from the Chinese American literature, Korean American literature displays oneness because most of Korean American writers attempt to concentrate on memories of Korea. With the foundation laid by general voices manifested in both Chinese and Korean American literatures, the book continues to inspect the groundbreaking work of *Mrs. Spring Fragrance* by the first Chinese American novelist Sui Sin Far, making comparisons with *East Goes West* by the first Korean American novelist Younghill Kang. The two figures remain unique among their peers in that both of them attempt to deconstruct and subvert the accepted thinking mode in the U.S. Unlike Sui Sin Far's counterattack of the thinking mode of exclusive discrimination, Younghill Kang challenges the American dreams represented by Benjamin Franklin and Ralph Waldo Emerson. Unlike most of Chinese American writers who mainly display the perspectives of ambassadors of goodwill, nostalgia, reminiscence, complaints, acculturation, the cultural transformation, protest against racial discrimination and appeal for acceptance and tolerance in the new land, Americanization and assimilability, Sui Sin Far deconstructs the thinking mode of exclusive discrimination by subverting racial stereotyped Other and displays the absolute difference between imaginary characters in Orientalism and the real Chinese immigrants so as to challenge the western cultural hegemony. While most of Korean immigrant writers of the first generation epitomized and mentioned Korea and the Korean patriotic spirit in their literature instead of Korean Americans in the U.S., Younghill Kang interrogates the life on the new land and manages to deconstruct two American dreams: Emersonian American dream — the spiritual utopia, and Franklinian American dream — the integrity of the family, the healthiness of competition in the society, the need for success and acquirement of material possessions.

The book comprises four chapters. After the brief introduction to the reasons why the study focuses on Chinese and Korean American literatures by the first-generation immigrant writers by 1965 under the umbrella term of Asian American literature, the angle of the book is determined on the basis of previous literary critics on Chinese and Korean American literatures in the U.S., China and Korea. With the scrutiny of genealogies of Chinese and Korean American immigrations and struggles embedded in the history, Chapter 2 will envisage the double-voiced discourses articulated in both Chinese and Korean American literatures by the majority of first-generation immigrant writers. Chapter 3 is devoted to interpreting deconstruction of exclusive discrimination thinking mode in *Mrs. Spring Fragrance* by Sui Sin Far and simultaneously analysis on deconstruction of two American dreams represented by Benjamin Franklin and Ralph Waldo Emerson in Younghill Kang's *East Goes West.* The last chapter is the author's conclusion based on the previous study of the representative works in the two branch fields of ethnic American literature.

Up to now, in Asian American studies, few critics from either Chinese or

Korean perspectives distinguish the self-expression of the writings by the first-generation immigrant writers from another. Thus, I attempt to present an alternative view to broaden the study field of Asian American literary criticism. The author intends to achieve this aim by making the best advantage of her direct native Chinese cultural background as a Chinese and her indirect Korean cultural background she comprehends as a student studying in the Republic of Korea as well as a detailed textual analysis of Chinese American literature and Korean American literature with the help of postcolonial literary theory. The book on Chinese American literature and Korean American literature might represent an initial attempt to fill in the gap.

Chapter 2

Double-voiced Discourses: Multiplicity in Chinese American Literature and Nationalism in Korean American Literature

The writings by most Chinese and Korean American writers of the first generation deliver double-voiced discourses. The first-generation Chinese immigrant writers manifest multiplicity on the one hand, and most Korean American writers display strong Nationalism on the other hand. Both Chinese and Korean immigrant writers of the first generation, from different perspectives, display the absolute difference between imaginary characters in Orientalism and the real oriental image. As nascent literatures, most of Chinese American writings display multiplicity as the ambassadors of goodwill, nostalgia, reminiscence, protests, complaints, Americanization and assimilability. Different from the Chinese American counterpart, most of Korean American writings show intense patriotism by exposing a collective trauma, the displacement from the ancestral homeland with yet an attachment to the home in term of custom, language and folk culture that exist consciously or subconsciously in the memory. The first-generation writers have great ability to go beyond the mere acceptance of the ideas they grew up with and become critical thinkers in the host land. Although the West does not receive other cultures as they are, these first-generation Chinese and Korean American writers are able to work out their own coherent ideas of how the world really works despite the mainstream society's brainwashing. Moreover, since few firsthand records are left by 19th-century Chinese immigrants, the writings of Chinese and Korean emigrants in America become precious documents which could test their effort to protest against racial discrimination and appeal for acceptance and tolerance in the new land. The shortage of formal records of this period makes these literary texts serve the function of documenting the social background that reveals the truth, and refute the image of the stereotyped Chinese emigrant in America as asserted by the dominant culture.

2.1 Multiplicity in Chinese American Works

The writings by the first-generation Chinese immigrant writers articulate the multiple voices: self-appointed ambassadors of goodwill, acculturation, protest against racial discrimination and appeal for acceptance and tolerance in the new land, reformatory view about how literature could serve political ends, sad wails by Chinese immigrants in the detention center on Angel Island, the cultural transformation of Chinese American literature in the new land based on the emigrant experiences in San Francisco Chinatown, and the plantation life, generational conflict and local affairs in Hawaii by first-generation Chinese students at the University of Hawaii. The writings emerged from the context of more than a century of persistent and deeply rooted racist descriptions of Asians in both official and mass culture as grotesquely alien others. Pressed to demonstrate the falseness of these representations, the first generation of Chinese American writers often attempted to present the true story.

Chinese American writing was born against a background of violent clashes between two races. As history is the foundation from which the texts have been produced in this period, the Chinese American historical background possesses a great value in both understanding and analyzing the texts. It serves to offer a background to, as well as a departure point for, the writings by Chinese American writers. As Elaine H. Kim points out, Chinese American writings, as a whole, function as a social statement and historical documents which reach beyond the realms of literary merits and artistic values. The problem of understanding Chinese American literature within its historical contexts is important because, when these contexts are not conversant, the literature is likely to be misunderstood and unappreciated. Consequently, literary study in this chapter is carried out with discussion of the chronological social historical background, with the intention of investigating how the literary devices reflect the varied experiences of the Chinese and Korean immigrants in the United State.

The history of the Chinese in America is riddled with expulsions, unfair taxes and labor practices, and most humiliating of all, exclusion laws directed at the Chinese and passed by state legislatures and the Congress of the United States. The U.S. Immigration Commission recorded the arrival of Chinese for the first time in 1820. A document in the National Archives in Washington gives the details of three sailors, Ah Sing, Ah Chuan, and Ah Cun, stranded in Baltimore by their shipmaster. They petitioned Congress for financial aid and lived for almost a year in the care of a merchant in the China trade named Levi Hollingsworth. Chinese footprints in

America were more and more recorded since then. Significant Chinese migration to the United States began with the California gold rush in 1848. This emigration continued unabated until 1882 when *the Chinese Exclusion Act* was passed.

Meanwhile, shortly after the war against Mexico and the annexation of California in 1848, Aaron H. Palmer, an American policymaker called for the importation of Chinese laborers to the United States and recommended Chinese laborers should be imported to build the transcontinental railroad as well as to bring the fertile lands of California under cultivation. "No people in all the East are so well adapted for clearing wild lands and raising every species of agricultural product… as the Chinese." (Takaki, 1989)[22] The vision of Chinese cultivating cane in Hawaii and building railroads and clearing lands in the west reflected a significant theme of American history — what the perspicacious scholar Perry Miller described as "the errand into the wilderness" because at the very beginning, the English settlement of America embraced a sense of mission — to remake a new world in their own image (Takaki, 1989)[23].

Except the ideological aspect, there is an economic one. The sugar planters in Hawaii calculated that capital would follow with getting labor first. During the second half of the 19th century, they ushered in a modern economy and made sugar industry obtain the big profit. To satisfy their demand for labor, planters made a thorough search of the world, mainly Asia in search of workers. In 1900, however, planters could no longer import Chinese laborers, for Hawaii had been annexed to the United States and federal laws prohibiting Chinese immigration had been extended to the new territory. Worried the Japanese were getting too numerous, and preferring to mix the labor races, they turned Korea to look for a new source of Asian labor because they wanted to compete against the excess of Japanese by importing Koreans and in 1903, they introduced Korean workers on the plantations. But the Korean labor supply was cut off when the Korean government prohibited emigration to Hawaii in 1905. To some extent, Chinese and Koreans were used to control and discipline Japanese workers for they demanded higher wages.

Like the planters in Hawaii, businessmen on the U.S. mainland cognized the importance to get the labor first. They regarded Asia as a new source of labor for American capitalism. Noting the need for Chinese workers for the railroads, agriculture, and manufacturing, San Francisco minister Otis Gibson reported in 1877 that there was a constant demand for Chinese labor all over the Pacific Coast because reliable white labor was not available at wages capital could afford to pay (Takaki, 1989)[28]. As a matter of fact, both Chinese laborers and Korean laborers were used as a transnational industrial reserve force and pitted against workers of other nationalities so as to break strikes and depress the wages of white workers.

These Chinese immigrant laborers, as sojourners, were hopeful that they would be able to work in a foreign country and return home rich in three to five years. They had two destinations — Tan Heung Shan which means Fragrant Sandalwood Hills in Chinese for the Hawaiian Islands and Gam Sann which means Gold Mountain in Chinese for California. In fact, China is a nation that had been deeply enlightened by the Confucian philosophy for thousands of years. Chinese people are influenced by teachings such as "remain content with your native land and try not to move away from it", and "every fallen leaf should return to its root". Consequently, for a man, to travel around leaving his family uncared was somehow a misdeed against the belief of piety and morality. Nevertheless, beginning in the 1840s and 1850s, they departed by the tens of thousands — about 46,000 to Hawaii in the second half of the 19th century and about 380,000 to the U.S. mainland between 1849 and 1930 (Takaki,

1989)[31]. Most of Chinese migrants to Hawaii and the U.S. mainland were from Guangdong, a province on the southern coast of China when sharp change took place in the 19th century.

Many factors contributed to the immigration of Chinese men to America in the mid-19th century. The reasons of this dramatic change might be categorized into three reasons as following: First, the economic breakdown in China made life more miserable. The Opium Wars of 1840–1842 and 1856–1860, and Sino-British Treaty of Nanking inflicted a sharp rising in taxation; meanwhile, a series of foreign treaties opened so important port cities to foreign power, which made the western business and goods pour into the China's market and thus shattered Chinese farm economy in the fierce competition. Second, social and political chaos, as well as domestic and foreign wars, especially the decade-long Taiping Revolution in the South, the Boxer Rebellion up in the North, and the bloody conflict between the Punti which means Local People and the Hakkas which means Guest People over possession of the fertile delta lands, endangered the reign of Manchu court, smashed the hope of retrieving a peaceful life. Third, the old law entry in Section 225 of Da Qing Lvli, which prohibited all the efforts of going and contacting abroad, was destroyed during the Taiping Revolution and the opening up of the port cities in the South gradually rid of people's dread toward other nationalities (Yin, 2000)[14]. Under such sociopolitical circumstances in the native land, they were forced to flee from their home country which was peopled with the violence and turmoil to seek sanctuary and wealth abroad.

Experiencing the internal disorder and poverty and then learning about the hard-won opportunities from Tan Heung Shan and Gam Sann, the younger people who were more impatient and more courageous left their villages for the remote lands. The majority of the migrants were married, illiterate or had very little schooling, but they dreamed of new possibilities inspired by stories about the gold mountains across the Pacific Ocean. In 1848, shortly after the discovery of gold at John Sutter's mill, a young man in Canton wrote to his brother who engaged in the tea trade in Boston:

> "Good many Americans speak of California. Oh! Very rich country! I hear good many Americans and Europeans go there. Oh! They find gold very quickly, so I hear... I feel as if I should like to go there very much. I think I shall go to California next summer." (Zo, 1971)[83]

Moreover, a witness in China described the excitement generated by the news of the gold rush:

> "Letters from Chinese in San Francisco and further in the country have been circulated through all this part of the province. The accounts of the successful adventurers who have returned would, had the inhabitants possessed the means of paying their way across, have gone far to depopulate considerable towns." (Takaki, 1989)[34]

As a result, Gam Sann promised not only gold to be mined but also chances for employment. Besides the poor peasants, the Chinese migration also included merchants — audacious businessmen seeking new opportunities for enterprise in the new world. The nature of the Chinese migration to the U.S. was mainly the movement of men as laborers, merchants, students, and a few rich knowledgeable people who usually hailed from the most privileged and westernized classes in China. Almost all of the Chinese migrants were men because single women did not travel alone to distant places, and married women generally stayed home as Confucianism defined the place of a Chinese woman.

Significantly, Chinese immigrants migrating to Hawaii instead of the U.S. mainland were more likely to take their wives with them than their counterparts who left for California. In 1900, "13.5 percent" of the Chinese in Hawaii were female while only "5 percent" of the Chinese on the U.S. mainland were female (Takaki, 1989)[35]. The specific phenomenon ascribed to, on the one hand, the ethnic differences between the two groups of migrants. The Chinese migrants in California were mostly Punti who practiced footbinding, whereas many of their counterparts in Hawaii were Hakka who did not practice footbinding. Accordingly, Hakka women had greater power than many Punti women to travel and work abroad. On the other hand, conditions and circumstances in the receiving country also regulated the difference in sex rations. In Hawaii, there were efforts to promote the migration of Chinese women because planters themselves realized that Chinese women could be taken advantage of controlling the Chinese laborers so that there would be less fear of riotous disturbances.

On the contrary, a combination of the missionary concern and employer self-interest that encouraged the immigration of Chinese women to Hawaii did not exist in California. As a matter of fact, the opposite case took place. Employers in California preferred a labor force of single men, a mobile work force ready to move to the next construction site or the next harvest readily and freely. They did not want to assume responsibility for Chinese families and care about the social needs of their workers. Therefore, their relationship with Chinese workers was contractual and businesslike, which prevented them from encouraging Chinese women migration to the U.S. Another probable reason is that Chinese male migrants in Hawaii could see that the work situation in the islands would be more settled and they would have been employed for five years on a particular plantation where they would live in a stable community. Accordingly, they were more likely to take their families with them to Hawaii. But in California, as miners or railroad workers or migrant farm laborers, Chinese men would be entering a frontier society where conditions would be difficult for their wives and children, which made them more unlikely to take their families with them. Moreover, Hawaii and the U.S. mainland implemented very different policies concerning the entry of Chinese women. While Hawaiian government exempted Chinese women and children from the quota in order to encourage them to come, the policies of the U.S. government, on the other hand, were designed to keep out Chinese women. The differences in state policies between Hawaii and the U.S. mainland not only determined how many Chinese women went to each place but also whether they migrated as wives or prostitutes. Unlike their sisters in Hawaii, most of the Chinese women entering California before 1875 were prostitutes (Takaki, 1989)[41]. As a result, the Chinese migration included only a few women, which was reflected in Chinese American literature.

Although the United States and China signed treaty of "peace, amity, and commerce" in 1844, which legitimated the Chinese to come across the Pacific Ocean to seek their fortune like newcomers from other parts of the world, the discriminative legislation of the 1853 *Foreign Miner's Tax*, and gradually shrinking mine resources forced many Chinese emigrants out of the gold fields. Thus, most of them moved to fill the void of low-paid labor created by America's rapid expanding industries and the Civil War. The most impressive contribution of Chinese emigrants was their work on the western section of the transcontinental railroad. These Chinese workers accounted for 90% of the railroad worker, who laid much of the tracks for the Central Pacific Railroad through the foothills and over the high Sierra Nevada. Their speed, dexterity, and outright perseverance were testimony to their outstanding achievements in construction of the most important American railroads in the 19th century. However, the United States Constitution made it impossible for Chinese emigrants to live as naturalized citizens in the States. In 1868, China and the United States signed the Burlingame Treaty, which simultaneously formalized immigration status for Chinese while denying them naturalization rights. Those who remained in America after this treaty were signed to find work in a variety of marginal industries against the language barriers and deep-rooted racial discrimination.

Some Americans did not welcome Chinese newcomers in the country. According to a document in California in 1862 —*An Act to Protect Free White Labor Competition with Coolie Labor*, and to discourage the immigration of the Chinese into the State of California, Chinese emigrants were perceived as a threat to white workers so that they should be regulated strictly in every way. During the nationwide depression in the 1870s, job competition became a hot issue. The Workingmen's Party led by Denis Kearney demanded a law to end Chinese immigration. Angry white workers rioted in protest of the alleged labor threat by Chinese workers. To the white settlers, even in the eyes of the newly coming poor Irish, Chinese emigrants are depicted as follows:

> "… considered physically small, dirty, and diseased. In manner, they were allegedly humble and passive, but also sneaky and treacherous. They

supposedly all looked alike and were depraved morally, given to theft, violence, gambling, opium, and prostitution." (Wu, 1982)[13]

Realizing the difficult situation in America, Chinese workers with little formal education and work experience scrambled together and retreated to the Chinese ghettos to seek relative security. Chinatowns, as a product of emigration and racial discrimination, provided Chinese emigrants with the social support networks that were not available to them anywhere else in the U.S. Chinatowns, to some extent, soon developed into a sub-system of government for Chinese emigrants in America.

In spite of the hard situation in America, Chinese emigrants kept moving to the United States in the following decades. *The Chinese Exclusion Act* was approved on May 6, 1882. It was the first significant restriction on free immigration in the U.S. history. It was also for the first time that federal law in the U.S. proscribed entry of an ethnic working group on the premise that it endangered the good order of certain localities. *The Chinese Exclusion Act*, along with the restrictions that followed, prevented the Chinese community from growing and assimilating into the U.S. society as European emigrant groups did. The difficulties of cultural and linguistic readjustment, in addition to the legal and conception barriers for the Chinese and their descendants, made the desire of return to China more idealistic than practical. Thus, the sense of guilt resulted from moving away from their country as well as the desire to go back constrained these Chinese to regard themselves as sojourners forever. Nevertheless, Chinatown's immigration records of San Francisco were all destroyed in the earthquake and fire in 1906. This provided the best opportunity for young male Chinese to take advantage of the loopholes in exclusion laws to enter America in disguise as paper sons. During the thirty years, a significant number of

Chinese emigrants were brought to America with fraudulent identity papers by reciting the coaching papers they got from San Francisco Chinamen who arranged this business specifically, while sometimes the real descents of the Chinese emigrants in America were denied entry because they did not prepare as carefully as the fake ones did.

Almost all of the above historical events are adopted in different literary texts by Chinese American writers. With the increase of the number of Chinese migrating to the United States, Chinese American writers has gradually become greater in amount. They started to write about their own ethnic history and culture, record their immigrant experiences and historical events in the new land, and explored through their writings the nature of their ethnic identity and gender identity.

Although Chinese Americans could be proud of a long and impressive literary history tracing back to the mid-19th century, Chinese American literature, like other marginal ethnic literatures, has long been ignored and discriminated against by the American literary canon. Although literary works have been defined as great art and as universal, according to the Eurocentric definition of universalism, only the works that manifest the white male American experience and cohere with the subjects of the white American literary tradition are deemed great and included in the American literary canon.

"Oriental", according to what Edward Said defines in *Orientalism,* means Western knowledge about the Orient and the knowledge of Orientals: their race, culture, history, traditions and society (Said, 1979)[38]. The identity of these Orientals, as Said believes, is not created by Orientals themselves, but by the West through "knowledge manipulations" (Said, 1979)[40]. Said suggests that the West does not receive other cultures as they are, "but as, for the benefit of the receiver, they ought to be" (Said, 1979)[67]. Said believes that Orientalism is a historically defined cultural and political fact (Said, 1979)[13]. Thus, the relationship between West and East is a relationship of Western power, domination, superiority, and writing over Eastern powerlessness, submission, inferiority, and silence. Consequently, Asian Americans were defined by the U.S. cultural imaginary as alien non-citizen, racial enemy, and colonized national (Lowe, 1996)[8]. The Asian males were seen as devious, timid, shrewd, and inscrutable while Asian females were thought to be mysterious, docile, submissive, and obedient, worthy of the label "model minority" (Cheung, 1993)[2]. The Asian men were coded as having no sexuality while the Asian women had nothing else (Kim, 1990)[69]. In this case, "the subject minority is conditioned to reciprocate by becoming the stereotype, live it, talk it, believe it, and measure group and individual worth in its terms" (Chin et al., 1974)[xxvii]. Therefore, anthologies of American literature largely consisted of the works by white writers. The literary canon has thus been used to maintain white cultural hegemony.

However, just as Gramsci believed that everyone, no matter what their occupation, their interests, or their education, is able to work out their own coherent ideas of how the world really works despite the hegemony as society's brainwashing, both Chinese and Korean immigrants have great ability to go beyond the mere acceptance of the ideas they grew up with and become critical thinkers. As a result, the situation has begun to change although the change is coming slowly. *The Chinese Exclusion Act* of 1882 labeled the severe era in Chinese American history in the United States, but Chinese American literature turned its first important page in forms of autobiography, short fictions and poetry that was scribbled on the wall of the detention center on Angel Island. These immigrant writers, from different perspectives, display the absolute difference between imaginary characters in

Orientalism and the real oriental image so as to reveal multiple perspectives of Chinese men and Chinese American women.

Most writings by the first-generation Chinese immigrant writers articulate their own voices by demonstrating multiple perspectives of their life in the U.S. The first voice is articulated by the self-appointed ambassadors of goodwill. "Ambassadors of Goodwill" is a term created by Elaine H. Kim in her *Asian American Literature: An Introduction to the Writings and Their Social Context* on classification of Chinese American literature (Wong, 1997)[45]. Lee Yan Phou, Wu Tingfang and Lin Yutang, who were the exempt class in the immigration injunction, belonged to the group of Ambassadors of Goodwill. These rich and knowledgeable people from the relatively upper class of China had the advantage to handle the English language in communication and in literary expression. They generally believed that if the misconception of the Americans to Chinese people and their culture was eliminated, they would be really exempted the targets of various forms of racial bias so that the American public would respect the Chinese and to be more sympathetic to China's misery. So the best way to clear up their dilemma was to unfold the real China and its civilization to the American public. These educated elites penned many books concerning charming stories of exotic food, dress, and ceremonies as a way to counter negative stereotypes and win friends in the West for China and the Chinese.

Lee Yan Phou manifested a glorious China in *When I Was a Boy in China* (1887), which was the first Chinese autobiography published in English in the United States, served as a preliminary encyclopedia to China, and found many readers in the West. He attempted to elucidate misunderstandings about China through his life story by purposefully equipping his book with the chosen facts on his own childhood experience to exhibit a live witness that overthrew the rumor about China and Chinese immigrants in the American mainstream society. He held a relatively just view on the two countries and their people. Therefore, he did not comment a lot on what is right or wrong, but only described everything vividly with a kind of light humor by referring to the counterparts in America. He effectively presented his China to the readers and left them to make their own judgment in such juxtaposition. Lee Yan Phou acted as an ambassador of culture for the most part of the autobiography. He made his tone pleasing to the readers and chose some exotic content in order to be accepted by the American public. He wrote with the hope that more Americans would get to learn about his China.

The other representative of self-appointed ambassadors of goodwill is Wu Tingfang who perceived the relationship between in the oriental and occidental civilization in many aspects in his works named *America through the Spectacles of an Oriental Diplomat.* Court official Yung Wing's *My Life in China and America* (1909) and Chiang Yee's *Silent Traveler in New York* (1950) are examples of Chinese commentary on the social inequalities existing in American society, including those inflicted on Chinese immigrants. Besides the stories of Chinese from the viewpoint of putative representatives, there was interest among American public in how America and Americans were thought by others. Americans viewed Asians as the inferior, which made it difficult for most readers to consider an Asian capable of the kind of comment on American life that Europeans from *Democracy in America* (appearing in two volumes: 1835 and 1840) and *The Old Regime and the Revolution* (1856) by the French political thinker and historian, Alexis-Charles-Henri Clérel de Tocqueville (1805–1859) to *Domestic Manners of the Americans* (1832) by the English novelist, Frances Milton Trollope (1779–1863) to *Letter from America* and *Alistair Cooke's America* by the British journalist, Alistair Cooke (1908–2004) were known for. American readers and publishers were more comfortable with tales of the exotic Orient than with Asian commentaries on anything American. In the preface to *Asian Commentary on America* in 1916, the editor warns that because "the masses of Americans do not take the Chinaman seriously… it will be difficult for the average American to conceive it possible that a cultivated Chinaman, of all persons, should have been honestly amused at our civilization." He encourages American readers to realize that some of "our fads and foibles held up as strange gods… [do seem] grotesque when seen in this yellow light" and warns them not to be offended by Chinese observers' comments about America and loyalty to China, because these are the "hallmark of actual novelty and [add] to the interest of the recital" (Graston, 1916)[vi]. However, the editor should not have worried about it because most Chinese writers wrote euphemistically about the West, and their critiques were generally tentative, apologetic and oblique.

Wu Tingfang (1842–1922), the Chinese magnifico and diplomat, wrote an English book under the title of *America through the Spectacles of an Oriental Diplomat* to state his perception on America and its culture. He was invited by an American friend to write about American and to speak of the people in an impartial and candid way. He thought that the Americans liked their "faults to be pointed out that [they] may reform" (Wu, 2002)[48]. As a keen and meticulous observer, he remarked such American aspects as its education, the paradoxical side of the American freedom, its governmental system, and American versus Chinese civilization. By comparing the similarity and difference in the oriental and occidental civilization in many aspects, he presented Chinese moral ethics, beliefs and life principles to the American readers, and called for "the doctrine of the universal brotherhood of men" (Wu, 2002)[96]. Comparing with Lee Yan Phou's China encyclopedia — *When I Was a Boy in China*, Wu pierced deeper under the surface in his seventeen-chapter panorama. He did more than his predecessor to make his cultural ambassador's goodwill more effectively achieved. The book served as a resourceful and highly readable document of the educated Chinese's views on both the United States and his homeland China at the turn of the 20th century. As a progressive and active politician, Wu Tingfang expressed his admiration toward a young and hopeful nation when facing the difficulty and drawbacks of his own old country. The core theme in the book is the good will of persuading the foreign readers understanding China, and the hope of developing friendliness with the west. As a result, Wu Tingfang started in Chinese American literature, in both English and Chinese, a tradition of observing, studying and commenting on the two giant nations.

Some works written by Americanized Chinese proposed the acculturation. One of the hot issues of the anti-Chinese sentiment in the United States lay in the Americanization of Chinese heathen emigrants. Against the Chinese unassimilation, the educated Chinese Americans expressed their dissatisfaction by claiming that it was the racial discrimination against the Chinese that made the incapability of Chinese emigrants to be assimilated into the American society. Yung Wing (1828–1912), a westernized Chinese who received a total western style education almost since the very beginning, depicted a prominent figure that was highly respected both in China and the U.S. in his autobiography of *My Life in China and America*. He disproved the American stereotype of Chinese unassimilation and xenophobia by illustrating the image of a hardworking Chinese American humanitarian. The book consisted of observations of and comments on the vital modern Chinese events and offered a unique perspective to view China and its culture under the given circumstance.

Yung Wing expressed the Chinese submissiveness fostered the aggressiveness and haughtiness of the ignorant westerners, and clung to education as the final solution to all problems in his works. Born in poverty, he went to America for education after several years of basic study in the missionary school in Macao and Hong Kong, and later graduated from Yale University as the first Chinese in 1854, and thus earned himself a reputation among the cultivated Americans as an admirable figure. Witnessing the successive failures of reformation and peasant uprisings in China, he concluded that education was the only way to save the ancient Chinese civilization from his personal experience and his acute observation of the east and west worlds. He wrote:

> "After our Chinese all receive the systematic education and enlightened by it to understand their rights, and realize they should morally and practically vindicate the public and personal rights, they will get rid of the stale notion and save their country from being partitioned." (容, 2003)[72]

According to the above quotation, readers easily discern that Yung advocates the significance of the government education in Chinese education history. As a person who received total western education and influence, Yung was already successfully Americanized and thought of himself as an American citizen who was under an obligation to his converted country. Because he was determined to be a good American citizen despite his firm will to serve his mother country, he was blamed by Frank Chin for having initiated a feminized, Christianized, and assimilationist tradition in his Chinese American autobiography. However, the importance of his autobiography is undeniable because it demonstrates early Chinese emigrant's efforts in acculturation and sets an active example for later emigrants in writing and in life.

Early Chinese American writings appeared soon after the large-scale immigration of the mid-19th century when numerous Chinese laborers were employed from villages and towns in southern China to build railroads and work in mines and on plantations in the United States. Answering the hostile environment, early Chinese immigrants expressed their protests and complaints in various oral and written forms. As a matter of fact, the early Chinese American writers were mostly an elite group because some Chinese immigrant merchants got education in schools in Hong Kong and Guangdong which were established by missionaries from the United States and other western countries after the 1820s. In addition, some Chinese young men were sent to the United States to study by American missionaries since the beginning of the 19th century. As a result, Chinese immigrants started to publish works in English in the 1850s because of the active participation by these Chinese merchants and students who were proficient in English.

These immigrants protested the institutionalized discrimination and maltreatment that they experienced in American society. One of the earliest and most influential works is *Letter of the Chinamen to His Excellency, Governor Bigler* penned by Hab Wa and Tong K. Achick in 1852 after California Governor John Bigler launched an anti-Chinese campaign for gaining support of his reelection in the early 1850s. The composition of the letter was organized by the leaders of San Francisco's Four Great Houses (the predecessor of Chinese Six Companies) and published in the two main newspapers in San Francisco — *Daily Alta California* and *San Francisco Herald*. To overthrow the accusation that Bigler posed on the Chinese as unlawful coolies and sojourners who stole fortune from America without gratitude and compensation back to it, and further state the Chinese merits and their contribution to the country, the letter argued that:

> "If you mean by 'coolies,' laborers, many of our countrymen in the mines are 'coolies', and many again are not. There are among them tradesmen, mechanic, gentry, and school masters… . None are 'coolies' if by that you mean bound men or contract slaves. The Chinamen are indeed remarkable for their love of their country… . They honor their parents and age generally with a respect like religion… many return home with their money… . But not all; others — full as many as of other nations — invest their grains in merchandise and bring it into the country and sell it at your markets… and how many are now returning to California as merchants who came over originally as miners." (Yin, 2000)[21]

According to the above excerpt, it is obvious that since most of the Chinese at that time were sojourners in America, the writers of the letter were a little evasive on the core issue that aroused resentment. In arguing they did not beat on it directly but stressed on the contribution the Chinese merchants and ordinary workers actually done to local economy. On Bigler's libel that the Chinese "are indifferent to the solemn obligation to speak the truth which an oath imposes", the letter refuted: "We do not deny that many Chinamen tell lies, and so do many Americans, even in Courts of Justice… . We pay our debts and are honest; and of course, tell the truth." (Yin, 2000)[21] The essay directly pointed out that it was the American exclusion and prejudice that drove the Chinese into the city ghettos without trying to get acquainted with Chinese culture and make some understanding first. Nevertheless, the economically sufficient merchants and other well-educated members strategically adopted a plea for tolerance instead of a face to face with Bigler.

Although the majority of the early Chinese emigrants were thought as subservient and amazingly tolerable to hard labor and misunderstandings, they tried defending themselves when outraged by racial mistreatment. "A Letter to San Francisco Board of Education" was written by Mary Tape to protest educational segregation in 1885. In the letter, Ms. Mary Tape wrote:

> "I see that you are going to make all sorts of excuses to keep my child out off the Public Schools… . Didn't God make us all!!! What right! Have you to bar my children out of the school because she is a Chinese Descend… . It seems no matter how a Chinese may live and dress so long as you know they Chinese. Then they are hated as one. There is not any right or justice for them." (Low, 1982)[44]

From the letter, readers easily find out that the equality advocated by American dream is a lie to the marginal Chinese American group. Thus, Mary Tape, who was a Chinese orphan from Shanghai and brought to the U.S. by missionaries at the age of 11, and grew up in a charity society, courageously challenged the education board directly in the letter appealing for opening education toward Chinese children and regarding people with Chinese ancestry equally. Her individual action was one of the many cases in which Chinese emigrant protested against racial segregation and other mistreatment. Although large numbers of Chinese emigrants in this period were uneducated rural workers, some of them managed to express their anger and ask for their rights in journals, newspapers and even appealed to court. Their writings were more outspoken and furious than the previously mentioned "writings for plea". Although there were some publications concerning Chinese emigrants, it is regretful that most of the ordinary Chinese were illiterate and not acquainting with literature so that they could neither fight with pens nor recording the historical facts in paper.

Furthermore, H. T. Tsiang's reformatory and activist works show another characteristic that contemplate how a transnational sensibility could find expression, how cross-racial and class-based alliances could be forged, how literature could serve political ends, and how one minority writer could attempt to reach a broad readership. H. T. Tsiang (1899–1971), a first-generation leftist writer in the United States, wrote one volume of poetry, three novels, and one play in English that represent pioneer works in the canon of Asian American literature because of his political awareness and bold use of literature as an instrument for social change. Following the principle of strategic appropriation from other writers, Tsiang created a new, hybridized literature supportive both of the international proletarian movement and the Communist cause in China by reworking formal and thematic elements from classical and contemporary Chinese literature, the proletarian works of 1920s and 1930s America, and western classics like the plays of William Shakespeare. Although few knows his work today, Tsiang is one of the earliest and most prolific innovators of Asian American literature, anticipating some of the appropriative methods, formal techniques, and critical strategies that have come to characterize the tradition and he is credited by Elaine H. Kim as the "first fictional rendition of the bachelor society in English by a Chinese immigrant" (Kim, 2006)[109].

His reformatory and activist works provide readers of Asian American literature with rich chances to pore over how a transnational sensibility could find expression, how cross-racial and class-based alliances could be forged, how literature could serve political ends, and how one minority writer could attempt to reach a broad readership. His published works manifest a broadly educated, idiosyncratically imaginative, and politically engaged mind at work on the challenges of his time. He fled to the United States to avoid arrest and possible execution in 1926. Committed to bringing about communism in China and dismantling capitalism everywhere, he found his desire and occupation in literature by which he hoped to message and sway readers not only to support his vision of a worker-centered Chinese state but also to change U.S. society itself. As a character in one of his novels declares, "With our paper bullets we shall change the direction of the wind", he believed that words could inspire revolution (Tsiang, 1931)[90]. He critiqued Japanese imperialism and American capitalism. Unlike the many whose writing never saw print, Tsiang ultimately did win the right to remain in the country and publish several books although the U.S. government repeatedly sought to deport him as an undesirable alien.

Tsiang's *Poems of the Chinese Revolution* (1929), focuses on the ongoing struggle for communism in China, argues that this revolution is related to a broader world revolution, and directs readers to ally themselves with diverse workers in the U.S. While working within a community of Chinese and American poets, Tsiang shared much in common with them so that his work sometimes engaged critically with theirs, participating in what Cary Nelson terms an "intertextual social conversation" (Mullen et al., 1996), Tsiang's *China Red* (1931) comments on Chinese and American politics and society by drawing from both Chinese and western traditions to trace the evolving political stances of two lovers separated by the Pacific Ocean during the late 1920s. In *The Hanging on Union Square* (1935), Tsiang remains interested in questions of political consciousness, but shifts his gaze from China to the United States by employing a much more experimental genre: the collective novel. For his third novel, *And China Has Hands* (1937), Tsiang focuses on urban America but stresses the diversity of its workforce and connectedness to developments in the Far East by appropriating and disrupting the conventions of romance. The shift from romance to activism of the couple in the novel parallels their turn from bourgeois fantasy to working-class consciousness, hence making *And China Has Hands* a standard, proletarian bildungsroman. Tsiang's last published work, the play *China Marches On* (1938), effectively dramatizes that national loyalty ought not to prevent people of different national origins from cooperating to challenge injustice. Like all of his works, Tsiang strongly suggests that individual desire and happiness must subordinated to the greater ideal of worldwide revolution against the interlocking systems of both capitalism and imperialism by combining thematic and formal elements from both Chinese and U.S. literary traditions in the novel.

As an innovator who incorporated Chinese literary traditions with western literary traditions, Tsiang is one of the only leftist authors of his time writing in English from a Chinese American perspective and is regarded as well-known writers because of his political awareness and bold use of literature as an instrument for social change. Although some readers may not always comprehend and agree with Tsiang's politics, we might respect his ambition and appreciate him as a creative figure that worked independently and adopted oriental and occidental traditions inventively.

Poetry on Angel Island manifests the angry poignant voices of frustrating wails, releasing ire, disappointment, homesickness and loneliness of these early Chinese immigrants in the detention center. The first-generation works in Chinese are inaccessible to Anglophone readers unless they are translated. Although some of the texts now regarded as landmarks in Chinese American literature history were in danger of being annihilated in the recent past, these once obscure works became one part of the Chinese American canon after they are translated into English and published in book form by the scholars and the community. One such work is the collection of *Island*: *Poetry and History of Chinese Immigrants on Angel Island, 1910–1940* consisting of poems written by detained immigrants on Angel Island in San Francisco Bay at the beginning of the 20th century, who carved into the wooden walls of barracks poems that expressed their loneliness at the harsh reception they had received in the U.S.

"Altogether more than 135 poems from the detention center have been recorded" (Lai et al., 1991)[23], 69 of which were published in the English translation form in the anthology *Island: Poetry and History of Chinese Immigrants on Angel Island, 1910–1940* edited by Him Mark Lai in 1991. The anthology consists of five parts which are concerned with "the voyage", "the detainment", "the westerners", "the thoughts", and "the deportees", respectively. All of the poems were written in the Chinese classical style with four lines or eight lines per poem. There were also versed and several couplets, even on long in the *pianwen* style. The subjects of Angel Island were concerning three aspects: First, explaining personal situations and expressing self-pity; Second, lament on the powerless actuality of China especially as compared to the other Asian countries such as Japan; Third, encouragement to the writers and those who came to this island after them. While there was only a few for encouragement, most of the poems were frustrating wails, releasing ire, disappointment, homesickness and loneliness. The poems are a vivid fragment of Chinese American history and a mirror reflecting an image of the past. In fact, there was no second emigrant group on which the unwelcome treatment was imposed as on the Chinese group.

These undated and unsigned poems inked or carved on the walls and floors of the bedrooms in the detention center by the Chinese applicants in Chinese characters expressed real feelings of overseas Chinese in such a perplexed environment. The angry poignant voices of these early Chinese immigrants compose a formidable counter discourse to the myth of America as a nation open to all immigrants. It left a treasure in Chinese American literature because they disclosed the truth of the unjust historical span which had been covered or omitted by the U.S. propaganda, and left the future generations a voice to be heard from the seemingly silent era.

Another poetry anthology called for the cultural transformation of Chinese American literature in the new land based on the emigrant experiences. The noteworthy poetry anthology is *JinShan geji*, which was later, selected into the English collection of *Songs of Gold Mountain: Cantonese Rhymes from San Francisco Chinatown* in 1987 by Marlon K. Hom. It represents the early immigrants' most sustained and distinctive literary production on American soil. Although they remained unknown outside of specialist circles until 1987, the poems were written by the class of literati in San Francisco Chinatown and were first collected in 1911 and 1915, ranging from Chinatown life and homesickness to China's republican revolution, from American hardships to fantasies of triumphant return to China, from the pain of family separation to the allures of Chinatown prostitutes, from support for Dr. Sun Yat-sen's Revolution of 1911 to outrage at the un-Confucian ways of emancipated women. These anonymous authors were most likely members of the better-educated merchant class who belonged to the exempt category under *the Chinese Exclusion Act*. These songs were composed in written form by members of poetry societies active in San Francisco Chinatown.

The prefaces to the two volumes of *Jinshan geji*, are key documents in the evolution of Chinese American literature. It called for the cultural transformation of

Chinese American literature in the new land based on the emigrant experiences because Gold Mountain poets' Cantonese origin made them use of dialect and American experiences which were not relevant to the homeland literati's rigid aesthetic standards any longer. There was an advocacy that Chinese American writings should be free from the traditional Chinese literary standards. The *Gold Mountain* songs' innovative mixture of Cantonese slangs, translations from English, and classical poetic diction is a compelling example of heteroglossia (Wong, 1997)[43].

Some university students represent the plantation life, generational conflict and local affairs in Hawaii. Such Chinese students at the University of Hawaii as James H. Chun, Phoebe Chun Chang, Wai Chee Chun Yee, and Li ling-Ai had been composing stories, poems, and plays about plantation life, generational conflict, and other local subjects in Hawaii since the 1920s. These writings were collected in *Pake* (1989), a special issue of *Bamboo Ridge: The Hawaii Writers' Quarterly* edited by Eric Chock and Darrell Lum to commemorate the two hundredth anniversary of Chinese immigration to Hawaii.

Most of these early immigrant writers used charming superficialities of food and dress, or ceremonies and customs, to appeal to the benign curiosity of the western readers, as they did during a period of severe discrimination. Accordingly, these early books exposed a marked dissociation between their authors and the common people. With few exceptions, these works ignored the large number of laborers recruited for agricultural and construction work in the United States. Their everyday life-and-death struggles of Chinese Americans under American domination were neglected by a small number of educated members who became representative spokespersons for the early Chinese immigrants in the United States.

There is one unique writer who, different from her contemporaries, depicts

Chinese immigrants sympathetically in the early stage of Chinese American literature. Edith Maude Eaton, whose pen name was Sui Sin Far, is the first Chinese American writer in English. She enriched Chinese American literature through her autobiographical account "Leaves from the Mental Portfolio of a Eurasian" (1909) and her short-story collection *Mrs. Spring Fragrance* (1912). She served as a link between past and future in that her works anticipated the post-World War Two works by other Chinese American writers such as Louis Chu's *Eat a Bowl of Tea* (1961), Frank Chin's *Chickencoop Chinaman* (1972) and *The Year of the Dragon* (1974), Laurence Yep's *Dragonwings* (1975), *The serpent's Children* (1984) and *Dragon's Gate* (1993), which exposed the false nature of the canonized picture of Chinese American history and the distorted images of the Chinese.

2.2 Nationalism in Korean American Works

> Every nation claims its own homeland, one which is described in the national literature, depicted in its art, and celebrated in its music. The homeland is not the mute object defined by physical geography; it is endowed with a personality and a moral character which complements and sustains the personality and moral character of those who inhabit it. The homeland is the ground in a near literal sense of national identity. It is significant that the land is conceived as a common possession, something all members of the nation share. (Poole, 1999)[16-17]

The nationalism as reflected in the literary writings by the first-generation Korean immigrant writers shows their exclusion and unassimilability in a host country on the one hand and their longing for home on the other. According to *American Heritage Dictionary*, the word "nation" or "nationalism" came from Latin *nasci*, which means "to be born", hence nation provides people with a starting point for family belonging, and it shows a nativity community, a nation-state of political significance, and as Rraymond Williams indicates: " 'Nation' as a term is radically connected with 'native.' We are born into relationships which are typically settled in a place. This form of primary and 'placeable' bonding is of quite fundamental human and natural importance." (Brennan, 1990)[45] As a storeroom for a collective memory, "native" provides Korean people with a certain nativism and identity. The first-generation Korean writers collect these memories in the books and other printed materials and intensify the formation of the nation that dreams of its freedom.

Most writings by Korean immigrant writers of the first generation by 1965 display the characteristic of nationalism by epitomizing Korea and the Korean patriotic spirit in their literature instead of Korean Americans in the U.S. The general characteristic of their work concentrates not on immigrant life but on memories of Korea, which casts its long shadow over their lives in the West. Korean American literature by the first-generation immigrant writers extends from the beginning of Korean migration at the beginning of the 20th century to 1965, with its termination being marked by *the 1965 Immigration and Nationality Act* which finally abolished the annual Asian immigration quotas. Referred to here as the phase of Asian estrangement, it depicts more than a half century of racial exclusion and cultural deprivation legitimized through institutionalized socio-economic and political practices. Unlike Chinese immigrants of the first generation, the Korean immigrants of the first generation confront double impact of U.S. racial discrimination and Japan's colonization. Moreover, unlike the Chinese, the Koreans lacked an economic foundation for ethnic solidarity, but they felt a strong sense of ethnicity which was even more intensely than the Chinese, and had source for community: powered by a unique necessity of struggling against Japanese colonialism in Korea. The strong sense of nationalism is revealed in their literature. Most of Korean immigrant writers of the first-generation center Korea, not about Korean Americans in the U.S. in their literature.

Korean American writing was born against a background of violent clashes between two races and severe domestic situation in Korea. The Korean American history should be taken into consideration for the sake of its great value in both understanding and analyzing the texts. Compared to that a number of Chinese emigrants immigrated in Hawaii and the U.S. mainland in the middle of 19th century, Korean immigrants of the first generation started to migrate to the United States half a century later.

Koreans, compared to Chinese emigrants, immigrated relatively late to the United States. The first group of Korean immigrants to the United States reached Honolulu in Hawaii as plantation workers in January 13, 1903 to fill in gaps created by problems with Chinese and Japanese laborers, while the Chinese immigrants started to arrive in Hawaii and the U.S. mainland in the 1840s and 1850s. Altogether some 8,000 Koreans sailed to the United States between 1903 and 1920. Setting off from the kingdom of Choson which means Morning Calm in Korean, the majority of them migrated to the territory of Hawaii. Like the Chinese migrants, the Korean migrants were young: more than 90 percent of the adults were between sixteen and forty-four. But unlike the group of Chinese immigrants, Koreans came from diverse walks of life, such as farmers, common laborers in the cities, government clerks, students, policemen, miners, domestic servants, and even Buddhist monks, most of who came from urban areas rather than the country. In their level of education, about 70 percent were literate, which was unlike the Chinese.

There are three main reasons that Korean people were grimly determined to leave their native land. First, converted to Christianity, many Koreans had been encouraged to emigrate by American missionaries. Significantly, 40 percent of Korean immigrants were Christians. Second, the Korean migration was also driven by political reasons: Hawaii represented a heaven from Japanese imperialism. The Japanese imperial government was controlling Korea at the time and the outlook toward the future was very poor. As a result, some Korean migrants left as political refugees, escaping from Japanese-government persecution in that the Japanese occupation was so severe and cruel for all Koreans. Hawaii was regarded as a place where Koreans could live on and struggle for national independence. Third, like the Chinese, Korean migrants were also pushed from Choson by poverty because dearth and drought had inflicted economic suffering.

From newspaper advertisements and posters, Koreans were given description of America as a land of gold, opportunities and dreams. Lured by fantasy and hope in the new world, Koreans started their migration which included many women: "of the 6,685 adults who entered between 1903 and 1906, nearly 10 percent were women" (Takaki, 1989)[56]. On the one hand, Korean men saw the islands as a place where family life was possible because they were guaranteed employment and housing on the plantations. On the other hand, many Korean men took their wives and children because they were afraid that they would not be able to return to Korea under Japanese domination. Moreover, an additional 1,066 Korean women came as picture brides during the next seventeen years. Korean migrants relied on Japanese agents to make the necessary arrangements for them. At the time of their marriages, the men were generally twenty years older than their picture brides who entered the United States with the Japanese passport issued to them as colonial subjects of Japan under the terms of the Gentlemen's Agreement. "By 1920, Korean women constituted 21 percent of the total Korean-adult immigrant population in the United State." (Takaki, 1989)[56] As a result, Korean community in the new land was not the same bachelor society as Chinese community.

However, in 1905, only two years after the arrival of the first Korean plantation laborers in Hawaii, Japan started to formalize its control over Korea by declaring it a protectorate. The Japanese government then prohibited Korean emigration to Hawaii because they wanted to curb Korean labor competition with Japanese workers in Hawaii and to cut off the source of Korean independence activities in the United States. Accordingly, Korean migrants arrived in much smaller numbers than the Chinese. Although Korean immigration to the United States had already started at the end of the 19th century, it was only after 1965 that significant numbers of Koreans began coming to the country because of *the Immigration and Nationality Act* in 1965 which finally abolished the annual Asian immigration quotas.

Social and political changes both in Korea and the United States could be reflected by the very history of Korean Americans in America. With the evolvement through emancipation from Japanese imperialism and the Korean War, and the changes of American immigration laws, the number of Korean Americans increased so that Korean Americans began to publish their stories in English since 1922 though the general public did not pay much attention to this phenomenon.

Unlike the Chinese immigrants of the first generation, the Korean immigrants of the first generation confront double impact of the U.S. racial discrimination and Japan's colonization. Although they left homeland for Hawaii and encouraged each other: "Kaeguk chinch wi" — "the country is open, go forward", Korean immigrants found the hardships and disappointments in the plantation world of Hawaii and thus many of them remigrated on to the mainland, working in the copper mines of Utah, the coal mines of Colorado and Wyoming, on the railroads in Arizona, the salmon fisheries in Alaska. "Most of them settled in California — some eight hundred out of a total Korean population of twelve hundred in 1910 (Patterson, 1977)[252]. Their mainland community remained small: Koreans numbered 1,677 in 1920 and only 1,711 twenty years later (Takaki, 1989)[270].

Unlike the Chinese, the Koreans did not have their own separate ethnic economy and community because they were too few in number to develop their own Korean town with its own stores, wholesalers, services, churches and commercial networks. Though they lacked an economic foundation for ethnic solidarity, the Korean immigrants felt a strong sense of ethnicity which was even more intensely than the Chinese, and had source for community: powered by a unique necessity of struggling against colonialism in Korea. This strong sense of nationalism is revealed in their literature.

Like the Chinese immigrants, Korean immigrants experienced widespread racial discrimination, ethnic antagonism. Moreover, the Korean immigrants were associated with the Japanese by whites and subjected to discrimination by the state. The Asian Exclusion League condemned both Korean and Japanese immigrants as undesirable aliens, and the San Francisco Building Trades Council demanded that *the Chinese Exclusion Act* be extended to the Japanese and Koreans. In 1913, *the Alien Land Act* prohibited Koreans from possessing land and limited leases in California, for Koreans had been denied naturalized citizenship.

Mainland Korean Americans was largely a community of chonggak (bachelors).

In the cities, they could work only as restaurant workers, gardeners, janitors, and domestic workers. Outside the cities, the overwhelming majority of Koreans were farm laborers and some of them were able to be employed as railroad laborers. For the Korean immigrants, economic success was tied to ethnic solidarity. The teams of Korean farm workers moved from one field to another field, depending on where they could find work. Gradually some Koreans were able to become farmers themselves by combining individual financial resource to lease and farm land. Instead of laboring on the edge of subsistence, some Korean entrepreneurial activities extended beyond agriculture. Koreans started to be extensively involved in the hotel business, restaurants, retail stores including groceries, tobacco shops, bakeries and photo studios, among which barbershops and laundries were the most popular enterprises. Like Chinese immigrants, "Koreans turned to self-employment as a route around racial discrimination in the labor market" (Moon, 1976)[199].

Though they were building a new Korean society in the new land by their diligent toil, they were unable to allow themselves to become permanent settlers. In the heart of the drifting Korean people was the struggle for Korean independence from Japanese occupation. Sojourners who left Choson became the person without a country because their homeland had been annexed by Japan in 1910. In fact, the first generation of Koreans in the U.S. suffered more mentally than the succeeding generations in that they were brutally detached from their father land. Grieving over their loss, the Korean migrants became even more tightly bound to their homeland and were driven by the need to free Korea from Japanese colonialism. Thus, life in America became to be organized around the independence movement and the nationalist movement gave many migrants a profound sense of purpose. They found community and identity in patriotic organizations and donated their profits to the patriotic cause. Churches were important engines of Korean nationalism and functioned as the religious arm of patriotic political organizations. A nationalist who lived in Los Angeles in the 1920s, Loiuse Yim noted: "The Korean's social life in the United States consisted of two main activities: politics and religion." (Yim, 1951)[167] Actually both served a common purpose.

The migrants' passionate patriotism held education in esteem because they believed that they could crush Japan with learning and their land could not belong to them without learning. As a result, Koreans on the U.S. mainland had the lowest illiteracy rate of all Asian immigrant groups — only 8 percent compared to 11 percent for the Japanese and 20 percent for the Chinese (Takaki, 1989)[279]. Meanwhile, Korean family life was also organized around the movement for Korean independence. Korean mothers raised their children as Koreans. Thus, home, family, church, and nation were organically integrated in the life of the Korean community. Anti-Japanese sentiments were pervasive in the Korean immigrant community in the U.S. Korean hatred for Japan became more and more intense as the migrants realized how they were cut off from the land of their birth. Korean migrants who had returned to their homeland were scared by Japanese oppression so much that they warned their countrymen in the U.S. to stay away from prison-like Korea.

Grieving over the loss of their homeland, Korean migrants felt a special mission to redeem their violated country. Their rage against Japanese colonialism exploded in 1908 when a Korean nationalist called Chang In-hwan assassinated Durham Stevens who was employed by Japanese government to calm American business fears of Japanese occupation of Korea and to convince the U.S. government that the Koreans themselves welcomed and benefited from the Japanese protectorate. Many Korean nationalists were driven by a patriotic fury. Most of the first-generation Korean immigrant writers mentioned and epitomized the Korean patriotic spirit in their literature.

Korean immigrant made great contribution to the Second World War. The Second World War was a watershed, a crucial dividing line in the history in the U.S. Although Korean and Chinese immigrants and their offspring had been viewed and treated as strangers across the Pacific Ocean, now they were asked to support their country in crisis and serve as Americans in the armed forces. As the United States confronted with fascism threat in both Asia and Europe, the nation had to extend it democratic ideals to immigrants of color and acknowledge its diversity. Furthermore, Korean nationalists felt that the long dream for national independence would soon become a reality, thus, in some degree, they welcomed the war, hopeful it would lead to the military destruction of Japan and the restoration of Korean independence. However, American government policies failed to distinguish the Koreans from the Japanese. After the U.S. declared war against Japan, the government identified Koreans as enemy aliens in that *the Alien Registration Act* classified Korean immigrants as subjects of Japan in 1940.

Korean immigrants were eager to attend to the war against Japan because many Koreans knew the Japanese language. They worked as Japanese-language teachers, translators of Japanese secret documents, propaganda broadcasters in the Pacific front and agents for underground activities in Japanese-occupied areas of Asia, etc. Korean involvement in the World War Two generated white-American respect for them. Koreans gained greater acceptance and had also helped to defeat Japan and free their father land.

Over past decades, historians and critics, such as Bill Ong Hing, Ronald Takaki and Lisa Lowe, to name only a few, have recapitulated Asian American immigration history which, as indicated by the title of Hing's book, *Making and Remaking Asian America through Immigration Policy 1850–1990*, has been prescribed by the U.S. exclusionist policy on immigration.[①] It is not the writer's intention to reiterate here the history of Asian Americans' radicalization and exclusion. Given the interrelation between the deficiency of the American democratic system and the predicament of Korean American literary discourses, it is investigated how the literary discourses by the first generation of Korean immigrant writers reflect and deconstruct the existence of racial alienation and abjection in the U.S. history.

In accordance with the place and the time, these Korean American writers derive from the four distinctly identifiable groups. First group consists of foreign students and political exiles that entered the U.S. between the early part of the 20th century and the mid-1960s. The second is composed of the children and grandchildren of Korean immigrants to Hawaii between 1903 and 1905, when American sugar plantation owners launched an intense though short-lived campaign to recruit Korean plantation labor. The third is formed from the children of immigrant farm and cannery workers in California and on the Pacific Coast in the early decades of the 20th century. The last comprises the children of the post-1968 immigrants, whose existence in the U.S. was made possible due to changes in U.S. immigration quotas in 1965.

The early Korean American articulated its voice largely in the form of autobiographies from the perspectives of educated exiles. The miserable history memory created postcolonial shadows that linger over Korean American writers of

① Bill Ong Hing, *Making and Remaking Asian America though Immigration Policy 1850–1990* (Stanford: Stanford University Press, 1991); Ronald Takai, *Strangers from a Different Shore: A History of Asian Americans* (Boston: Little, Brown and Company, 1998); and Lisa Lowe, *Immigrant Acts* (Durham: Duke University Press, 1996).

the first generations. These shadows, along with Korea's colonial past also signal the failure of the American state to make room in the national family for the racialized figure of marginal ethnic group. In this early stage, the Korean immigrant's writing is rooted in the socio-political factors in Korea that trigger dissatisfaction in their father land.

During the second half of the 20th century, a succession of the first-generation Korean intellectuals immigrated to the United States, starting with a small number of political exiles who arrived shortly after Japan's occupation of Korea. Then several thousand foreign students continued to arrive after additional U.S. legislation excluding laboring immigrants from Asia passed in 1924. The Korean immigrants increased greatly when the U.S. immigration policies strongly favored educated Asian immigrant professionals and technicians in the early to middle of 1970s. These Korean immigrant intellectuals created relatively few literary works in English, while they produced many Korean American writings in Korean which could be found in many volumes of self-published poetry, as well as in occasional and periodical journals. Ch'oe Yun-hong asserts that the immigrants cannot be "literary" because their lives are too stressful and filled with suffering, adding that if they could really write about their immigrant lives, they would win the Pulitzer Prize (Ch'oe, 1989)[64]. However, Korean American writings in Korean could be found in three issues of the journal *Jip'yongsun* (Horizon), which were published from 1973 to 1976, the *Miju Hankuk Munihyopho*e (Koreans in America literary association)-sponsored journal, *Mijumunhak* (Korean American literature), which produced issues from 1981 to 1985.

Except these journals written in Korean, Korean immigrant writers in English are few and tend to be people who came to the United States as students and have lived in this country for decades. Most of their works concentrate not on immigrant life but on memories of Korea, which casts its long shadow over their lives in the West. Among the writers in Korean American literature in this period, the best known was Younghill Kang (1903–1972) who was considered to be the father of Korean American literature. He wrote two interconnected novels, *The Grass Roof* (1931) and *East Goes West* (1937). While Japanese colonization was a target in the first, the second described Chung-pa Han's experiences in his new home — the United States. Younghill Kang's world is an immigrant bachelor society. Besides Younghill Kang, there are two other men writers of the first generation in the early period — Richard E. Kim and Ty Pak, and two women writers named Sook Nyul Choi and Mary Paik Lee.

Rather than writing fiction on Korea Americans in the host country, Richard E. Kim, as one young Korean intellectual immigrant in the U.S., expresses his strong sense of patriotism by only recording the past and the lost in his native land. His personal experience in northern Korea and Manchukuo bears the imprint in his works. He was born in Korea in 1932. He was raised first in Korea, and then Manchuguo, which was a puppet state located in what is now Northeast China and Inner Mongolia and governed under a form of constitutional monarchy. The area, collectively known as Manchuguo, was designated by China's erstwhile Qing Dynasty as the "homeland" of the ruling family's ethnic group, the Manchus. Then he came back to Korea again. His childhood consisted of living during the tail end of Japanese occupation. After serving in the army, he was honorably discharged as first lieutenant, Infantry in 1954 and came to the United States in 1955. His life in both Korea and China, his childhood in Japan's colonization and the Korean War (25 June, 1950–27 July, 1953) left its indelible mark on Richard E. Kim and thus shaped his sensibilities. As a student in the University of Iowa writing program, he wrote his first novel, *The Martyred* (1964), which was a critically acclaimed bestseller about the Korean War, and was also nominated for a National Book Award. It was followed by *The Innocent* (1968), about politics in the postwar Republic of Korea, and *Lost Names: Scenes from a Korean Boyhood* (1970), a collection of stories.

Richard E. Kim inquiries into such vital questions as the human conscience and the meanings of evil, suffering, and the truth in Korea during the Korean conflict in his *The Martyred*. The narrator, Captain Lee is sent to interview the two survivors after twelve Christian ministers are found dead. Lee hopes that one of them, Reverend Shin, will confess betraying his colleagues so that Lee could use it to discredit them and arouse the support of the Korean Christians for the war. As a matter of fact, Reverend Shin was spared because unlike the others who died like dogs, pleading for mercy, he refused to grovel and denounce his faith. However, instead of telling the truth, he falsely confesses the betrayal and, after being forgiven, becomes a popular preacher who deliberately preserves the people's false image of the fallen ministers as "martyrs", recognizing that his parishioners are already burdened beyond their abilities by the war and that he loves them too much to destroy their faith. The novel concerns such sensitive questions as the war, Korean Christianity, and the juxtaposition between the large-scale suffering of the public during wartime and the individual aspects of faith, hope, confession, etc. Although the story is built around the twelve murdered ministers, Richard E. Kim returns to the suffering of the innocent Koreans as a whole, thus implicitly posing the question of whether the people of Korea are just as much "martyrs" as the twelve murdered men (Oh, 2007)[181]. The novel was immensely popular, staying on the *New York Times* Bestseller List for twenty weeks and being translated into ten languages (Fuse,

2001)[162]. It was "a nominee for the National Book Award" and for the Nobel Prize in literature (Han, 1996)[146]. Few first novels have met such critical success as *The Martyred* which remains the only work by an Asian American ever nominated for a Nobel Prize in literature. Richard E. Kim rose to fame overnight and became one of the best-known Koreans in the West, which in turn assured him reputation in the Republic of Korea as well. Pearl S. Buck, the first American woman who won the Nobel Prize in literature, wrote a promotional statement for Richard E. Kim. While the issues conducted in *The Martyred* brought Richard E. Kim critical and popular success in 1964, his second novel, *The Innocent* (1968), was attacked by critics.

In his second work of *The Innocent*, Richard E. Kim continues to reflect on such issues of his native country as "the difficulty not only of rebuilding the nation after a horrific war, but also of maintaining one's innocence amidst so much corruption and in the face of the continued momentum of wartime violence" (Oh, 2007)[126]. It dealt with the events surrounding a military *coup d'etat* in the Republic of Korea and delineated the ethical dilemma encountered by a group of army officers as they realize that morality may require them to do horrific deeds. "This novel was not as successful as *The Martyred*, perhaps because it was published during protests against the Vietnam War, and enthusiasm for Kim decreased as a result." (Fuse, 2001)[162]

On the one hand, most of the critics considered unconvincing the depiction of military men in the Republic of Korea as decent, moral leaders struggling to save their country from corruption. On the other hand, the book's primary defenders were rightists, who asserted that the book was garroted, clubbed, shot in the back of the head drawn, quartered and pushed over a high cliff by the liberal book review establishment because of its negative depiction of softheaded liberalism and because it presents a disturbing essay on the Asian mind and spirit at the very moment when the U.S. intellectuals were groping to make sense of the actions of the South Vietnamese military. However, Richard E. Kim asserted that *The Innocent* was created for readers in the Republic of Korea instead of Americans and insisted that *The Innocent* was not about the 1962 military coup but about such universal human problems as ethical, moral and corruption issues. The military, where country boys learned how to drive cars, operate machinery, learn organizational skills, improve discipline, and obtain expertise, might, to some extent, be the only instrument or institution of modernization and have a certain role to play at that time. However, many readers in the Republic of Korea viewed the book and Richard E. Kim as supporting the military, which was becoming disreputable for its excesses, abuses and brutal repression of citizens from the 1960s to the 1980s.

Richard E. Kim's third book, *Lost Names: Scenes from a Korean Boyhood* (1970) still focuses on his experiences in a time of anguish during the Japanese occupation of Korea. *Lost Names* is a useful and rare book whose title came from the grim fact that the Japanese Pacific War policy forced the Koreans to renounce their own names and adopt Japanese one instead. A young boy recounted one Korean family's experience during the war years. Although *Lost Names* is technically a novel, all the characters and events described in the book are real, but everything else is fiction. In this classic tale, Richard E. Kim paints seven vivid scenes from a boyhood and early adolescence in Korea at the height of the Japanese occupation, 1932 to 1945. Richard E. Kim has said:

> "Koreans have lost so much. Things have been taken away, but we have also lost things ourselves. In Korea, we are always exhorted to rail against

> the bad guys who take things away. But did we do something dumb ourselves that feeds into our loss? In *Lost Names*, there are Japanese atrocities; but there are also Korean collaborators. My grandfather used to say that he shed no tears over the demise of the Korean royalty because they were rotten through and through; he just felt sorry that it had to be Japanese and not Koreans who got rid of them." (Kim, 2004)[5]

Rather than writing fiction about Korean Americans, or about contemporary Korea, Richard E. Kim turned later to translation, television documentary work in the Republic of Korea, and published a book of photographs. He once said: "I never intended to be a writer; I wanted to be a student of history. I am obsessed with the past, with all the things we have lost. I want to remember them, to record them, to think about them." (Kim, 2004)[6] Thus, his statement explains his shift to other forms of expressions.

Another Korean immigrant writer Ty (T'ae Young) Pak concerns his old country by delineating how the past national memory in the native land haunts the present life in the new world. Since he was born in Korea in 1938 during World War II, Pak experienced Japanese colonial rule, Korea's liberation from Japan in 1945, the division of Korea during the subsequent U.S. and Soviet occupation, and the trauma of the Korean War at his home country during his early childhood and young adolescent years. After he received his law degree from Seoul National University in 1961, Pak worked as a reporter for the English dailies *The Korea Republic* and *The Korea Times*. He immigrated to the United States in 1965, and received his Ph.D. in English from Bowling Green State University, Ohio in 1969. From 1970 to 1987, Pak taught in the English Department at the University of Hawaii and decided to retire early and devote himself to writing at the age of 49. His first collection of short stories, *Guilt Payment*, was published in Hawaii in 1983 and was widely adopted as textbooks at many U.S. colleges.

Ty Pak underscores the incongruity between a Korean American's present life in the U.S. and his past life in Korea. In the title tale, the characters are an immigrant father who is a middle-aged college teacher and now safely ensconces in a middle-class suburb in Honolulu, and his cranky daughter who wants him to pay for a costly music education in Italy. She invokes her deceased mother, which triggers her father's miserable memories of the war. Thus, an apparently ordinary life in the U.S. poignantly contrasts with the terrible and violent past in Korea. The father recalled how he wanted to escape and save himself when his baby daughter's crying threatened to expose his hiding place to the enemy soldiers while his wife, who refused to abandon the baby, was killed.

Although both the father and the daughter survived to live in another world in another age, the past never passes and continues to harass the present and the future. Pak's views of the world were deeply affected by his war experiences in Korea when he was young. His world is mostly male-centered war and adventure stories, which is similar to Younghill Kang's immigrant bachelor society and Richard E. Kim's exclusively male military world. The worlds of these Korean immigrant male writers are all male-centered, to some extent. Moreover, in Pak's male-centered and action-oriented exciting stories, the disturbing and nauseous manifestations of misogyny could be detected. Pak often depicted his female characters as seductive objects of male desires, female avengers, shrieking shrews, shamans possessed by spirits, and frightening vampires. His female characters were raped, tortured, maimed, and mutilated in one story after another.

Except the above male writers who indulge themselves in the topic related to the native Korea, some female writers also express their longing for home in Korea and link their individual experiences to their national memory. In contrast with works about the male worlds that make little mention of the fates of women or carve them into the victims or the undervalued, women are central characters in work by Sook Nyul Choi. Sook Nyul Choi was born in Pyongyang in 1937. During the Korean War, she fled to the Republic of Korea. She emigrated to the U.S. to continue her higher education. After receiving her B.A. from Manhattanville College in 1962 and becoming a school teacher in New York, she moved to Cambridge, Massachusetts, where she began working as a writer, lecturer, and creative writing teacher.

According to her Korean war experience in the first half of 20th century, she created her first novel of *Year of Impossible Goodbyes* (1991), which relates the story of a young Korean girl named Sookan and her family as they struggle to survive under the foreign occupations of the Democratic People's Republic of Korea in the Second World War. The writer addresses an enduring issue — what is the price of freedom — by depicting what happens when families live under a dictatorship that classifies them as second-class citizens because of their ethnicity and essentially puts them in slavery. Choi's expresses the unflagging spirit of the Korean nation to confront the tyranny of the Japanese and Russians during and after World War II. She introduces an oft-overlooked portion of World War II and the years beyond — Korea's occupation by Japan and ultimately America and Russia splitting the country in two. The story happens in the spring of 1945 in the village town of Kirimni, on the outskirts of Pyongyang and ends with the family's dramatic escape to the Republic of Korea, thanks to the courage of her relatives, especially Aunt Tiger. With great clarity and fluid prose, Choi details the Japanese Imperial Army's occupation of Korea with martial force during the Second World War and the subjugation of the Koreans at the mercy of the brutal Japanese army and afterward the incoming Russians.

Through her subtle observations, Choi charts the fear, sadness, and strength of the Korean people. Against a historical canvas, Choi employs a simple but often poetic language to tell a gripping story that leads to her eventual flight to freedom. Though it is told from a child's perspective, readers gain an understanding and knowledge of the horrific global expanse of the Second World War as they enter the lives of the Choi family and experience the devastations the war wrought on the Korean populace. In laying to rest the past that is impossible to forget, Choi immortalizes the strength of a nation that refused to relinquish to its identity. Bridging the gap between cultures and time periods, this prominent multicultural novel could serve the purposes of studying and discussing the mistakes of history, the tolerance of culture, and the resolve of the human spirit. The book won numerous awards including Best Books for Young Adults, ALA Notable Book and Judy Lopez Book Award by the National Women's Book Association. It has been translated into several languages including Korean, French, Italian, and Japanese. It is also available in Braille and in audio book.

Echoes of the White Giraffe (1993) is a sequel to *Year of Impossible Goodbyes*. Sookan, the heroine who fled war-torn Seoul with her mother and younger brother in Choi's *Year of Impossible Goodbyes*, returns in this haunting sequel to tell the life as a refugee in the Pusan area of the Republic of Korea two years after the start of the Korean War. The family is again separated by the Korean War. Escaping falling bombs, Sookan, and her mother arrive safely on the outskirts of Pusan, uncertain of the whereabouts of the men. They establish themselves in a shack at the top of a mountain where, along with throngs of other refugees, they try to restrain their doubts and intense sorrow as they tackle daily routines, face their memories, and dare to hope for a secure future. Now at the age of 15, Sookan manages to set up a sense of normalcy during turbulent times as she goes to a makeshift school and worries about her missing father and older brothers. Sookan experiences her first romance. She takes comfort in her blossoming yet forbidden friendship with the handsome Junho, sharing with him her hopes and dreams of a happy, peaceful future. After the truce is signed ending the war, the surviving family members are reunited. Noticing that the men discuss work, school, and international events while the women gaily bustle in the kitchen, Sookan decides that she cannot be satisfied with family life and traditional female roles. She asks herself why she "always felt so empty restless, and incomplete." "What was I searching for? I didn't know exactly, but I felt I had to go away to find something that would fill the emptiness inside me." (Choi, 1993)[115] Sookan has been dreaming about going to America anyway and immerses herself in her schoolwork and achieves her goal of attending college in the U.S.

Choi speaks with an authentic voice, both in describing a young girl's coming of age and a war-weary nation where, even today, people are uncertain about the fate of family members. She has once again managed to put a nobody on a tragic episode of world history. This inspirational work possesses a confident and quiet triumph with universal reverberations. Moreover, Choi suggests that Sookan is forced to leave because she is able to see the limitations that both she and other women in Korean society have to confront with, even though they could exhibit extraordinary courage and strength during periods of social upheaval. For Sookan, one representative of typical Korean women, fulfillment, resolution, and completion are not possible in Korea. She runs away from these restrictions and boards a plane to America.

Choi's books tie literature into the social studies and explore themes of communism, freedom, international politics, and interaction among nations. In both of her novels, the United States of America is regarded as a promised land. In *Year of Impossible Goodbyes,* the family members anxiously wait for the Americans, whom they expect will deliver them from Japanese colonization. Listening to the recordings of "Clementine," "Swanee River," and "Home on the Range," Sookan imagines the U.S. as a holy place where she will not feel empty, restless, and incomplete any longer.

Some journals in Korean express their nationalism and the indefatigable spirit of the Korean nation by the three groups of Korean immigrant intellectuals, who immigrated to the United States in three phases respectively, starting with a small number of political exiles shortly after Japan's occupation of Korea in 1905, continuing after the exclusion of laboring immigrants from Asian in 1924, and then when American immigration policies strongly favored educated Asian immigrant professionals and technicians in the early to mid-1970s. Although Korean immigrant intellectuals have created relatively few literary works in English, Korean American writings in Korean could be found in three issues of the journal *Jip'youngsun* (Horizon), which were published between 1973 and 1976, and the *Miju Hankuk Munihyophoe* (Koreans in America literary association)-sponsored journal, *Mijumunhak* (Korean American literature), which produced only four issues between 1981 and 1985. Others to publish Korean American writings in Korean include two volumes of *Chaemi Si-in Jakp'umjip* (Collected Korean American poetry, 1989 and 1990), which was published by the Los Angeles-based Korean Poets Association of America, and a 1988 issue of *Munhaksegye* (The literary realm 1, No.1, Spring 1988), which includes some poetry and short stories in English.

Both Chinese and Korean immigrant writers of the first generation, from different perspectives, articulate their own voices and display the absolute difference between imaginary characters in Orientalism and the real oriental image so as to reveal multiple and diverse perspectives of Chinese men and Chinese American women beyond the Western imagination. They paint a grim picture of the immigrant exiles, suspended between two worlds and lacerated by feelings of inferiority. Since the relationship between West and East is a relationship of Western power, domination, superiority, and writing over Eastern powerlessness, submission, inferiority, and silence, Asian Americans were defined by the U.S. cultural imaginary as alien non-citizen, racial enemy and yellow peril. These immigrant writers subvert racial stereotypes and binary opposition so as to present and restore the living experience of Asian immigrants by challenging the authoritative images and theories from multi-dimension angles and undermining the surface or apparent meaning of American dreams advocated by Benjamin Franklin and Ralph Waldo Emerson.

A small number of educated elite members became representative spokespersons for the vast majority of Chinese in the United States, which is very paradoxical because until recent decades the vast majority of Chinese in the U.S. were laborers, laundry and restaurant workers or domestic servants. The writings by the first-generation Chinese immigrant writers manifest various perspectives: self-appointed ambassadors of goodwill, acculturation, protest against racial discrimination and appeal for acceptance and tolerance in the new land, reformatory and activist's view about how literature could serve political ends, sad wails by Chinese immigrants in the detention center on Angel Island, the cultural transformation of Chinese American literature in the new land based on the emigrant experiences in San Francisco Chinatown, and the plantation life, generational conflict and local affairs in Hawaii by the first-generation Chinese students at the University of Hawaii.

The majority of Chinese American writings manifest the characteristic of multiplicity. First, some Chinese works, whether they are autobiography or imaginative writings, have the same purpose of introducing Chinese culture to the world, explaining the real Chinese and China to the west and bridging the gap in understanding between East and West. These elites intend eagerly to verify that Chinese are good citizens in the world of the WASP's civilization, and seek acceptance in this unwelcoming society under the special circumstance. Although these ambassador writers more or less bend to satisfy the American readers with an exotic oriental flavor in tone and contents, the progressive thinking and action with the literary efforts made by them have already challenged western prejudice against China. The other characteristic in the works by the first-generation Chinese immigrant writers is the acculturation proposed by some Americanized Chinese Yung Wing, a westernized Chinese who received a total western style education almost since the very beginning. One of the hot issues of the anti-Chinese sentiment in the United States lay in the Americanization of Chinese heathen emigrants. Against the Chinese unassimilation, the educated Chinese Americans expressed their dissatisfaction by claiming that it was the racial discrimination against the Chinese that made the incapability of Chinese emigrants to be assimilated into the American society. Another characteristic by Chinese emigrants in the U.S. during the 19th century is evidence of their efforts to protest against racial discrimination and to appeal for acceptance and tolerance in the new land by an elite group of merchants and students who were proficient in English. Furthermore, as a first-generation leftist writer in the United States, H. T. Tsiang's reformatory and activist works show another characteristic that pore over how a transnational sensibility could find expression, how cross-racial and class-based alliances could be forged, how literature could serve political ends, and how one minority writer could attempt to reach a broad readership. Moreover, poetry on Angel Island manifests the fifth characteristic: the angry poignant voices of frustrating wails, releasing ire, disappointment, homesickness and loneliness of these early Chinese immigrants in the detention center. Another notable characteristic in the first-generation immigrant works is that a poetry anthology called for the cultural transformation of Chinese American literature in the new land based on the emigrant experiences by members of the better-educated merchant class in poetry societies then active in San Francisco Chinatown, who belonged to the exempt category under *the Chinese Exclusion Act*. The last characteristic in the first-generation immigrants' works is the representation of the plantation life, generational conflict and local affairs in Hawaii by Chinese students at the University of Hawaii.

According to the above multiplicity, it is easy to discern that the first two categories of works by educated members, who became representative spokespersons for the early Chinese immigrants in the United States, used charming superficialities of food and dress, or ceremonies and customs, to appeal to the benign curiosity of the western readers, as they did during a period of severe discrimination. Accordingly, these early books exposed a marked dissociation between their authors and the common people. With the last five categories, these works highlight the large number of laborers recruited for agricultural and construction work in the United States. Their everyday life-and-death struggles under American domination were manifested in various walks of life.

Similarly, the early Korean American literary articulated its voice of nationalism largely in the form of autobiographies from the perspectives of educated exiles. Unlike the beginning of Chinese American literature in the 1850s, Korean American literature by the first-generation immigrant writers starts from the beginning of Korean migration at the beginning of the 20th century. The miserable history memory created postcolonial shadows that linger over Korean American writers of the first generation. In this early stage, the Korean immigrants' writing is rooted in the socio-political factors in Korea that trigger dissatisfaction in their father land. These Korean immigrant intellectuals created relatively few literary works in English, while they produced many Korean American writings in Korean which could be found in many volumes of self-published poetry, as well as in occasional and periodical journals. Except these journals written in Korean, Korean immigrant writers in English are few.

The immigrant writings address the 800,000 Korean Americans who are lonely and facing many hardships on the host land. There are several common themes that weave through the early Korean American literature. One is the wish of writers to pass on their experiences by introducing Korean culture to the next generation who could not experience life in Korea. The other theme reflects the conflict between race and nationalities colored with sensibilities particular to Korean culture. Another is concerning the crisis of identity which derives directly from Korean history and culture. The last is that some Korean writers wrote euphemistically about the West, and their critiques were generally tentative, apologetic and oblique. Korean immigrant writer Park No-Yong's *An Oriental View of American Civilization* (1934) was an example of Korean commentary about American life.

Among the writers in Korean American literature in this period, Younghill Kang was considered to be the father of Korean American literature. Besides Younghill Kang, there are another two men writers — Richard E. Kim and Ty Pak, and two women writers named Sook Nyul Choi and Mary Paik Lee of the first generation in the early period. Besides three issues of the journals by Korean Americans in Korean, their literary expressions manifested their unflagging nationalism from the four diverse aspects.

First, Richard E. Kim created an exclusively male military world, the Korean War, politics in the postwar Republic of Korea, and experiences in a time of anguish during the Japanese occupation of Korea. Rather than writing fiction about Korean Americans, or about contemporary Korea, Richard E. Kim, in the U.S., wrote for readers in the Republic of Korea instead of Americans. Then, Ty Pak displays the male world deeply affected by the war experiences and underscores the incongruity between a Korean American's present life in the U.S. and the past in Korea. Even as a Korean immigrant in the new world, he finds that the past never passes and continues to harass the present and the future. Pak's views of the world were deeply affected by his war experiences in Korea when he was young, which also represents and reflects most of Korean Americans' inner world. His world is mostly male-centered war and adventure stories, which is similar to Younghill Kang's immigrant bachelor society and Richard E. Kim's exclusively male military world. Third, in contrast with works about the male worlds that make little mention of the fates of women or carve them into the victims or the undervalued, the lives of women are focused on Sook Nyul Choi's writings. In the world of Korean women, the writer addresses an enduring issue — what is the price of freedom — by depicting what happens when families live under a dictatorship that classifies them as second-class citizens because of their ethnicity and essentially puts them in slavery. Choi's book expresses the unflagging spirit of the Korean nation to confront the tyranny of the Japanese and Russians during and after World War II. Choi studies and discusses the mistakes of history, the tolerance of culture, and the resolve of the human spirit by immersing literature into the social studies and exploring themes of communism, freedom, international politics, and interaction among nations. In both of her novels, the United States of America is regarded as a promised land. Last, another woman writer, Mary Paik Lee contains the majority of the 20th century and displays a vital cultural viewpoint on the last century from the perspective of an Asian-American woman's life from childhood through old age in *Quiet Odyssey: A Pioneer Korean Woman in America*, one of the few memoirs by an Asian American woman, and the only memoir by a Korean American woman. She manifests Korean nationalistic pride, the sacrifice by the older generation for the younger generation, the violent loyalty to the family, the burning satisfaction Korean women derived from hard physical work with resilience and characteristic grace. She opens a window into an important era for Korean Americans, offers testimony of the Korean immigrant families' experiences in the adopted land, and provides a social commentary about what America and American life has been.

According to the above category, early Korean American literature inevitably ponders on the issues relevant to Koreans back in Korea (specifically the Japanese occupation, the Korean War and political strife through the eighties), and later speculates issues of dealing with their immigrant experiences. The history of Korean American literature, to some extent, is the history of the Korean immigrants overcoming numerous difficulties in their process of immigration to the United States. The worlds of these Korean immigrant male writers are all male-centered.

Moreover, some books written by women writers focus on men: her father, her brothers, and her sons, which is not surprising, in consideration of Korean identity has been traditionally defined as male-centered.

There are two main differences between Chinese and Korean American Literatures by the first-generation immigrant writers by 1965. First, although it is desirable to discuss Chinese American literature and Korean American literature together in one book, the result is unbalanced in the number of works and the points of view in literary expression in that there are many more examples of Chinese American literature, undoubtedly because the Chinese American community experienced a longer history and furthermore there always has been a larger proportion of English-speaking Chinese American writers than Korean American writers in the early stage. The number of Korean American population was only a small portion of the severely restricted Chinese population. As a result, it is no wonder that there was the relatively small number of published Korean American writings in English compared with that by Chinese immigrants and Chinese Americans in this period. Another reason is that the two groups of Chinese immigrants and Korean immigrants come to the new land in different periods: with the first arrival of Chinese in 1820, beginning in the 1840s and 1850s, the Chinese immigrants departed by the tens of thousands — about 46,000 to Hawaii in the second half of the 19th century and about 380,000 to the U.S. mainland between 1849 and 1930; a succession of the first-generation Korean intellectuals immigrated to the United States in three phases respectively, starting with a small number of political exiles who entered the adopted land shortly after Japan's occupation of Korea in 1910s, then continuing with several thousand foreign students who arrived after the exclusion of laboring immigrants from Asia in 1924, and increasing greatly when American immigration policies strongly favored educated Asian immigrant professionals and technicians in the early to mid-1970s. Different arrival times shaped the layers and communities of Asian Americans. Moreover, both international and American circumstances change with alteration inside the two countries of China and Korea in different time periods. Thus, the number of writings and multiple points of view vary in Chinese American literature and Korean American literature in their own early stages.

Second, Korean American literature by the first-generation immigrant writers manifests a stronger sense of unflagging nationalism than Chinese American literature. Korean American literature was rooted in the particularities of Korean American social history though Korean American writing emerged from the very American context shared by Chinese American group. The earliest Korean American writing came out into view when persistent racial discrimination had been deeply rooted in both institutions and mass ideology for almost one century and a half. The sequelae of American racial discrimination and Japan's colonization of Korea greatly narrowed the growth of Koran American communities for six decades. Except the slow growth of the population, political and economic developments in Korean American communities were hindered by the double colonization of Korean immigrants because they were unable to resort to their motherland for trade or diplomatic assistance as other immigrants in the United States did. The trauma of Japanese occupation had so long-lasting effects that lots of Korean American writers continued to manifest their extreme distress of the exile deprived of the sustaining illusion of triumphant return to their dreamy homeland after a life-long toil in a hostile land. As a result, long after the Japan's occupation was formally ended in 1945, Korean American writings went on to express the trauma that Japanese colonization caused. Korean American writers from New Il-han, Younghill Kang, and Richard E. Kim to Kim Rongyoung, Theresa Hak Kyung Cha, and Sook Nyul Choi depicted the effects of Japanese colonization on Korea, Korean people, Korean immigrants, and Korean Americans. This anxious feeling gradually become delicate in Korean American writing until only now, almost eight decades after World War Ⅱ.

Although the highly diverse individual voices of Chinese American writers and Korean American writers are reducible to no single measure, their recurrent themes and techniques reflect psychological and cultural dilemmas specific to Asian Americans. These writers spiritually witness routine social brutality, tell stories about and for those previously left out of the literary and social text, make claims for the powerless, and reveal the courage and resourcefulness of people generally believed to be invisible and inarticulate.

Chapter 3

Double-voiced Discourses in Sui Sin Far and Younghill Kang

The general characteristics of the Chinese American literature demonstrate multiplicity and Korean American literature displays a strong sense of nationalism. Two distinctive figures in the two branches remain unique among their peers in that both of them do not follow the routine line but attempt to deconstruct and subvert the accepted thinking mode in the U.S. Sui Sin Far counterattacks the thinking mode of exclusive discrimination and Younghill Kang challenges the American dreams represented by Benjamin Franklin and Ralph Waldo Emerson. Unlike most of Chinese American writers who mainly display the perspectives of ambassadors of goodwill, nostalgia, reminiscence, complaints, acculturation, the cultural transformation, protest against racial discrimination and appeal for acceptance and tolerance in the new land, Americanization and assimilability, Sui Sin Far deconstructs the thinking mode of exclusive discrimination by subverting racial stereotyped Other and displays the absolute difference between imaginary characters in Orientalism and the real Chinese immigrants so as to challenge the western cultural hegemony. While most of Korean immigrant writers of the first generation epitomized and mentioned Korea and the Korean patriotic spirit in their literature instead of Korean Americans in the U.S., Younghill Kang interrogates the life on the new land and manages to deconstruct two American dreams: Emersonian American dream — the spiritual utopia, and Franklinian American dream — the integrity of the family, the healthiness of competition in the society, the need for success and acquirement of material possessions.

3.1 Deconstruction of the Thinking Mode of Exclusive Discrimination in *Mrs. Spring Fragrance*

As the first person of Chinese descent in the United States to write and publish work about Chinese-American life, Sui Sin Far produces the first stories about Chinese American life, records their ethnic experience in the new land and draws an original and realistic picture for them in her *Mrs. Spring Fragrance and Other Writings* (1912). Unlike most Chinese American writers in her period, she has no intention of appealing to the curiosity of the American reading public, acting as an ambassador of goodwill, and manifesting of nostalgia, reminiscence, Americanization and assimilability. Sui Sin Far's stories conduce to awakening feelings of retrospection, empathy and sympathy in the White readers so that the consciousness of binary opposition of race could be deconstructed, to some extent. She attempts to deconstruct the binary opposition in race, subvert the state-sanctioned stereotypes of Chinese people, and expose racial discrimination jeopardy so as to construct a utopian world where people of all races live harmoniously with the idea of universality of human nature as its core and one family as its form. She forces

American nationals to observe and consider the world of Chinese immigrants in a fresh way so as to change these immigrants' state of being in exotic places. *Mrs. Spring Fragrance*, notable for being "the earliest book of fiction published in the United States by an author of mixed Chinese and white descent", discusses issues of racism, assimilation, and the alienation of Chinese Americans in North America, particularly from a woman's point of view (Hsu, 2011)[9]. *Mrs. Spring Fragrance* focuses upon such characters of early Chinatowns as women and children who were omitted from depictions of the Chinese bachelor societies that were formed when women were prohibited by *the Chinese Exclusion Act* from traveling from China to join their husbands in America. Other themes include the conflict between tradition versus modernity experienced by immigrants and the change of lifestyle many were forced to make in a new country, the difficulties faced by the children of mixed-race marriages — an issue close to Sui Sin Far's own experience — and the prejudice against these marriages expressed by both the Chinese and white American communities.

Asian American literature started with two Anglo-Chinese sisters. Two Asian Americanist scholars Amy Ling and Annette White-Parks established Edith Maude Eaton and Winnifred Eaton as "the first Asian North American writers of fiction" (Ling, 1995)[21]. The two founders were not equally appreciated when they were alive and after they passed away. Edith Maude Eaton exhibited portraits of turn-of-the-20th century Chinese Americans with an insider's sympathy, gave voice to the inarticulate Chinese American women and children and deconstructed the state-sanctioned stereotypes of silent and invisible yellow peril, while Winnifred Eaton catered to the readers by writing the popular Orientalia in her time. Although Edith Eaton produced only one book-length volume: a collection of short stories published in 1912 under the title of *Mrs. Spring Fragrance*, Asian American criticism tends to see Edith Maude Eaton, who adopted the Chinese pseudonym Sui Sin Far and embraced her Chinese roots, and wrote sympathetically about Chinese immigrants in an era when many were quick to become as American as possible, as a conscientious social critic. Winnifred Eaton, on the other hand, who faked herself an identity of Japanese-English background, wrote under the fabricated Japanese pseudonym Onoto Watanna and enjoyed a successful career writing popular Orientalia in her time, is regarded as a sellout and a race traitor though she wrote at least a dozen popular and popularly acclaimed novels from 1899 to 1922. Edith Eaton, who enjoyed what was at best a mildly successful career when she was alive, has received much more initial scholarly attention after her death, whereas Winnifred Eaton, a writer who was successful in her own lifetime, has attracted only a few scattered articles and dissertations nowadays.

Edith Maude Eaton (1865–1914), a Chinese-British-Canadian-American writer, was the first person of Chinese descent in the United States to write and publish work about Chinese-American life and was well-known for her writing about Chinese people in North America and the Chinese American experience in the U.S. All her life, she devoted herself to fight against the discrimination against Chinese Americans in the white society. As a result, when she died in 1914, her contemporary Chinese Americans placed a tombstone, caved with four large Chinese characters: Yi-Bu-Wang-Hua (a righteous person who never forgets Chinese and China), to express their gratitude and admiration. Annette White-Parks calls her "the foremother to the women writers of Chinese ancestry… to whom such contemporary writers as Maxine Hong Kingston and Amy Tan look for roots" (White-Parks, 1995)[6]. She was also regarded as "spiritual grandmother" of Maxine Hong Kingston

(Ling, 1990)[120].

"Sui Sin Far", her pen name, is the Cantonese pronunciation of fragrant Water Lily that symbolizes purity in China and narcissism in the western tradition. Most critics of Sui Sin Far interpret that Eaton chose the name not only because of the beautiful image of the flower, but she purposefully took the meaning of the two words: sin and far, which suggest the division from other people and conflict within her Eurasian identity, and embody her difficult and agony as well as the marginal status of herself and her people. Sui Sin Far using such a typical Chinese pen name, to some extent, indicates her choice of identity, which leads her whole life to contribute to Chinese Americans although she found herself an outsider both in Chinatown and in the Anglo-American neighborhoods where she was raised when she came to the United States from England as a young girl in the early 1870s.

The reason that Sui Sin Far, from the perspective of an insider, recorded the ethnic experience of Chinese Americans and gave voice to the inarticulate yellow peril derives from her own experience. Born in Macclesfield, Cheshire, England, Sui Sin Far was the eldest daughter of an Englishman named Edward Eaton, a merchant who met her Chinese mother while on a business trip to Shanghai, China. Her mother was Grace "Lotus Blossom" Trefusis, the adopted daughter of English missionaries. Her parents' mixed-race union was very rare in an era when Chinese were considered a low race and openly discriminated. Sui Sin Far was the oldest daughter and second child of fourteen children. In the early 1870s, her family left England to live in Hudson, New York, United States, but stayed there only a short time before relocating to Montreal, Quebec, Canada. Because of the poverty in the large family, at a young age, Sui Sin Far left school to work in order to help support her family. She worked as an English teacher in a Chinese Sunday school in 1894 and she took a job as a correspondent for *Montreal Daily Star* in the following two years. Then she replaced her younger sister Winnifred Eaton in Kingston, Jamaica as a full-time reporter for *Gall's Daily News Letter*. Eaton started writing as a young girl; her articles on the Chinese people were accepted for publication in Montreal's English-language newspapers, the *Montreal Star* and the *Daily Witness*. Although her natural appearance and manners allowed her to easily pass as an Englishwoman, she asserted her Chinese heritage and wrote articles on what life was like for a Chinese woman in white America. As Dominika Ferens said, "Sui Sin Far's reporting experiences had heightened her awareness of institutionalized race and class inequalities and authorized her to speak her mind on public affairs" (Ferens, 2002)[8]. Thus her fictional stories about Chinese Americans first published in 1896 were a reasoned plea for her society's acceptance of working-class Chinese immigrants in the time when the United States Congress maintained *the Chinese Exclusion Act*, which officially and legally prohibited Chinese immigration to the United States. With the ensuing years of efforts, Sui Sin Far finished her first and only collection of linked short stories — *Mrs. Spring Fragrance*, which she mentions as the production of her "lifelong accumulation of experience, ideas, network building and purposeful struggle" (White-Parks, 1995)[196]. Since its publication, *Mrs. Spring Fragrance and Other Writings* has been favorably reviewed and won critical and popular acclaim, just as Yin Xiaohuang wrote: "Quaint, lovable characters are the Chinese who appear in these unusual and exquisite stones of our Western Coast — stories that will open an entirely new world to many readers." (Yin, 2000)[86]

The collection offers more than mere chinoiserie: Sui Sin Far's questions concerning love, tradition and the meaning of assimilation in a new nation are still resonant almost a century later. These short stories in the collection are separated into two parts, one of which is *Mrs. Spring Fragrance* for adults, and the other of which contains twenty stories for children, collectively known as *Tales of Chinese Children.* Set in Seattle and San Francisco in the U.S., they manifest the endeavors and delights in the daily lives of immigrant Chinese families in North America. Particularly poignant are the stories depicting the cultural conflicts of Eurasians and recent immigrants.

Essentially, as a woman writer with mix blood, Sui Sin Far expresses a lot more ambivalent and sophisticated emotions than those having single and integrated identity through the depiction of the survival conditions of Chinese Americans. Though facing with conflicts and confrontations as her protagonists in the stories, she firmly believes that she could deal with the cultural conflict and live with two identities, namely her Chinese identity and English one, simultaneously. She wrote in her autobiography of *Leaves from the mental Portfolio of a Eurasian* (1909): "After all I have no nationality and am not anxious to claim any. Individuality is more than nationality… I give my right hand to the Occidentals and my left to the Orientals, hoping that between them they will not utterly destroy the insignificant connecting link." (Eaton, 1995)[230]

Unlike her Chinese peers whose works act as the ambassadors of goodwill, nostalgia, reminiscence, Americanization and assimilability, Sui Sin Far's writings deconstruct racial stereotypes and display the absolute difference between imaginary characters in Orientalism and the real Chinese immigrants so as to challenge the western cultural hegemony in the following part. She subverts the state-sanctioned cognition by deconstruction of the thinking mode of exclusive discrimination and reconstruction of a utopian world as one family will be probed by rereading *In the Land of Free* and *The Story of One White Woman Who Marries a Chinese* in *Mrs.*

Spring Fragrance. No matter who you are, and no matter where you are from, all human beings have common ground in human nature and meanwhile possess their own specific ethnicity. Human beings are selves existing as individuals, who can have their own character and habits; they also exist as social beings and must live in a community because the individual free development relies on the free development of all human beings.

In *Mrs. Spring Fragrance*, Sui Sin Far deconstructed the thinking mode of exclusive discrimination by subverting the stereotyped literary images. The background of *Mrs. Spring Fragrance* is in the late 19th century and the turn of the 20th century, when the WASPs harbored the thought pattern of exclusive discrimination based on the binary opposition in race, and meanwhile, the Chinese immigrants crossed over the Pacific Ocean and fled from calamitous China to earn fortune in the new world. Binary opposition is, in fact, ethnocentrism with the pseudo-scientific theoretical foundation of scientific racialism. The ethnocentrism and scientific racialism provided the pseudo-scientific theory foundation for the superiority of whites and the inferiority of specific ones, which resulted in proceeding to racial discrimination in various social aspects such as institution, culture, and literature, etc. As a cultural deployment of rational practicality for WASPs to define and contain the yellow other, racial stereotyping started as soon as Chinese entered the United States in the mid-19th century.

Grounded in the white Anglo-Saxon Protestants' assumption of their superiority, the discourse has coined a series of stereotypes of Chinese Americans. The superior race of white Anglo-Saxon protestants was civilized, sophisticated, or as postcolonial critics put it, metropolitan, whereas, Chinese immigrants and Chinese Americans, like other ethnic minorities, were defined as inhumane, barbarian, backward, underdeveloped, dangerous and mysterious beings. Silence is another feature which is labeled on Chinese Americans. The Whites judged another culture solely by the values and standards of their own culture. The ethnocentric individual judged other groups relative to his or her own particular ethnic group or culture, especially with concern to language, behavior, customs, and religion. These ethnic distinctions and subdivisions serve to define each ethnicity's unique cultural identity. This phenomenon could be termed as ethnocentrism. which is "the habit of seeing things only from the point of view of one's own group" and "judge one culture by the standards of another culture" (Anderson et al., 2006)[63]. William G. Summer defined it as "the technical name for the view of things in which one's own group is the center of everything, and all others are scaled and rated with reference to it" (Merton, 1996)[248]. He further characterized it as often leading to pride, vanity, beliefs of one's own group's superiority, and contempt of outsiders. Sudesh Mishra describes that "surely there is a label that carries differences between human body (clothes, language, and dinner custom) and mentality" (Sudesh, 2002)[21]. Americans or the Caucasians took this label for granted, believing that they were superior to other races in both physical and mental aspect, which is quite cruel and unequal to other ethnic groups. The belief considers that white people to be superior to people of other racial backgrounds. As Frank Chin and Jeffery Paul argued in their essay "Racist Love," white racism enforces white supremacy (Kostelanetz, 1972)[65]. To Frank Chin and Jeffery Paul Chan, white supremacy is "a system of order and a way of perceiving reality. Its purpose is to keep whites on top and set them free" (Kostelanetz, 1972)[65]. Thus, white supremacy in a way means racial supremacy, so whites' influence on minorities intensifies their self-contempt.

Moreover, a pseudoscience of scientific racism prevailed in the late 19th century and at the turn of the 20th century. It is a term seldom used today but which has a long and ignoble history in the modern world. In the late 18th century, the renowned scientist and philosopher Christoph Meiners published his famous treatise *The Outline and History of Mankind.* Central to his analysis was a qualitative comparison of peoples by race — a comparison which his own popularly-accepted findings claimed revealed a clear hierarchy. With the now-discredited science of phrenology, Meiners described whites as being endowed with clear superiority to all races in both their intellectual as well as moral faculties. As influential as it was, Meiner's work was par for the course in the institutionalized science of racism of the age. It denied facts to build and defend a false thesis about superior race and inferior race though, today, there are a lot of great scientists that proves the opposite, namely, there is no superior race and all human races had the same origin.

Scientific racism denoted the use of scientific, or ostensibly scientific, findings and methods to support or validate racist attitudes and worldviews. It was based on belief in the existence and significance of racial categories, but extended this into a hierarchy between the races to support political or ideological positions of racial supremacy. Scientific racism was most widespread during the New Imperialism period in the second half of the 19th century. These theories often worked in conjunction with racism. It asserted that there was a link between race and intelligence, as well as hierarchically classifying races, hence claiming the superiority or inferiority of specific ones. Scientific racism alleged that scientific evidence showed significant evolutionary differences between races or ethnic groups.

Furthermore, Carolus Linnaeus (1707–1778), a Swedish botanist, physician and zoologist, who laid the bases of binomial nomenclature (the method of naming species) and is known as the "father of modern taxonomy" (the science of describing, categorizing and naming organisms) was also a pioneer in defining the concept of "race" as applied to humans. Within Homo sapiens he proposed four taxa of a lower (unnamed) rank. These categories are, Americanus, Asiaticus, Africanus, and Europeanus. They were based on place of origin at first, and later skin color. Each race had certain characteristics that were endemic to individuals belonging to it. Native Americans were reddish, stubborn, and angered easily. Africans were black, relaxed and negligent. Asians were yellow, avaricious, and easily distracted. Europeans were white, gentle, and inventive. The early examples and theories of scientific racialism provided the pseudoscientific theory foundation for the superiority of whites and the inferiority of specific ones.

Consequently, based on the white Anglo-Saxon protestant's assumption of their superiority, the hegemonic discourse created a series of stereotypes for Chinese immigrants and Chinese Americans. Since the WASPs had a belief that only their Anglo-European culture was civilized, sophisticated, or as postcolonial critics put it, metropolitan, Chinese Americans, like other ethnic minorities, were defined as barbarian, backward, underdeveloped. Since their culture was more highly advanced especially in technology, the WASPs regarded themselves as the center of the world whereas the Chinese Americans as the margins. Since the WASPs regarded themselves as the embodiment of what a human being should be, the proper Self, Chinese Americans were Other, different and therefore inferior. This practice of judging all who are different as inferior is called "othering" which is a term coined by Gayatr Chakravorty Spivak. It is a psychological operation upon which colonialist ideology depends. It refers to the practice of judging all that are different as inferior. Racism, sexism and classism, are all specific forms of othering (Tyson,

1999)[36].

Besides exclusive discrimination, ethnocentrism and scientific racism, in the late 19th century, there did exist various forms of racism, and one of them was institutional racism, which Lois Tyson referred to "as the incorporation of racist policies and practices in the institutions by which a society operates" (Tyson, 1999)[382]. As a result, institutional racism left so indelible imprints on Chinese immigrants that they were even reduced to feeling shameful for themselves, which Guan Hefeng expressed in her book. "Chinese Americans feel themselves to be inferior, less attractive, less worthwhile, and less capable." (Guan, 2007)[88] Under white supremacy background, different minor ethnicity was unable to be put in an equal position because the evolution of ethnic groups was not complete in the Whites' eyes. The mainstream of American society discriminated against Chinese immigrants who were brought to America in large numbers with the name of contractual laborer from the late 19th century. Especially after completing the transcontinental railroad across the American continent, they were refused to join American nationality and were not allowed to marry another race. Meanwhile, in order to restrict Chinese to come to American for the Gold Rush, the American Congress in 1882 passed *the Chinese Exclusion Act*. All Chinese who came to America were subjected to a lengthy inquisition.

As a cultural deployment of rational practicality for WASPs to define and contain the yellow other, racial stereotyping started as soon as Chinese entered the United States in the mid-19th century. In the American hegemonic discourse, Chinese image was constructed for the WASP's sake. Popular stereotypes at the turn of the 20th century were the heathen Chinee and the yellow peril. The heathen Chinee was created in the poem under the title of "The Heathen Chinee" as a parody of Swinburne's "Atlanta" by Bret Harte, who portrayed a Chinese Ah Sin winning at cards over two white gamblers by cheating, which manifested that the heathen Chinee was peculiar for dark ways and vain tricks. The yellow peril was a phrase Jack London adopted for the title of a book — *The Yellow Peril* (1904). WASPs had a nightmare that the fecund Chinese, awakened to western mechanization by Japan, would invade and overwhelm the Caucasian race.

The yellow peril was epitomized in the stereotypical images of Doctor Fu Manchu and Detective Charlie Chen, who underscored the emasculated stereotypes of Chinese male immigrants. The image of Fu Manchu created in 1913 by British author Sax Rohmer was suspected of being a gay, who had mastered western knowledge and science and turned them to satanic abuse and thus represented the terror of the yellow peril for the American public. He embodied the primordial Chinese evil without moral and compassion, totally dedicated to pure intellect and impersonal projects of human sacrifice. Frank Chin describes him in this way:

> "Dr. Fu, a man wearing a long dress, batting his eyelashes, surrounded by muscular black servants in lion cloths, and with his habit of caressingly touching white men on the leg, wrist, and face with his long fingernails is not so much a threat as his frivolous offense to white manhood." (Chin, 1972)[60]

Charlie Chen, however, as a product of racism, was described by Biggers as a womanized bumbling detective who solved murders for his white masters:

> "He was very fat indeed, yet he walked with the light dainty step of a

woman. His cheeks were as chubby as a baby's, his skin ivory tinted, his black hair close-cropped, and his amber eyes slanting." (Biggers, 1925)[76]

Thus, according to the above detailed descriptions of Doctor Fu Manchu and Detective Charlie Chen, Chinese men were figured in the West as being in some sense feminized, dependent and passive. The western perception of the Chinese male was really a product of the self-representation of western man that depended on an inferior other to construct his identity in a dualistic fashion and to justify his pathological assumption of masculinity as pure strength and mastery. This is what Edward Said calls Orientalism, a special form of othering. To consolidate the self, western orientalists invented the orient as its other. By defining Chinese Americans as cruel, sneaky, evil, cunning, dishonest, and the like, WASPs defined themselves as kind, straightforward, good, upright, honest, and moral, which was in contrast to the imaginary oriental they created. As a matter of fact, the stereotypes for Chinese Americans are an invention of the WASPs, as a contrast to which they have been able to define themselves positively and justify their political and economic oppression of the Chinese immigrants and Chinese Americans. These racist images as the result of fear, ignorance and xenophobia are popular, disseminated and encouraged in American mainstream culture because WASPs feared that the increasing myriads of Chinese Americans, who were willing to work long hours at difficult tasks with the lowest pay, posed a great threat to employment opportunities for WASPs.

Similar to their white sisters and male compatriots, Chinese American women have long suffered the burden of Euro-American stereotypes. They bear several layers of oppressions in the society. In patriarchal society, women function as a subaltern class that has been defined and silenced by the dominant culture. Living in the United States, a multi-racial country dominated by the male WASPs, with white hegemonic ideology and discourse in the dominant position, Chinese American women stooped in an awkward position on the marginal belt of the margin. Accordingly, as ethnic minority females, Chinese American women were excluded from mainstream culture and from centers of power in their own Chinese community. They are facing with social taboos from both worlds that belittle their authentic experiences so that they often find themselves inarticulate and being silenced simultaneously by both the mainstream WASP's male society and the traditional Chinese patriarchal culture. Following the patriarchal perception of white women either as an angel in the house like Miss Esther Summerson in *Bleak House* by Charles Dickens or a mad woman in the attic like Rochester's wife Bertha Mason in *Jane Eyre* by Charlotte Bronte, and the traditional European perceptions of Chinese people as a model minority or the yellow peril, Chinese women have been shaped into a similarly bifurcated roles: the China Doll or the Dragon Lady who was a character created by the popular newspaper comic pictorial serial "Terry and the Pirates" in the 1930s.

Like their counterpart of the white angel in the house, the China Doll is demure, modest, devoted and deferential. Following her man ten steps behind, tittering behind her ivory hand, with her eyes always downcast, she performs as a magnificent manipulated puppet, a sexual object and submissive servant who is never taken seriously by both white men and Chinese men. At the opposite side of the spectrum is the Dragon Lady, a mad woman in the attic, and a female counterpart to the diabolical Fu Manchu. This dangerous and treacherous woman has talon-like six-inch fingernails, and she could poison a man as easily as she seductively smiles and puffs on her foot-long cigarette holder. The stereotype of Chinese and Asian women as the rotten and seductively charming sex slaves of white men has been ingrained in American consciousness by numerous Hollywood epics and dime novels. Even nowadays Chinese women are frequently approached in terms of these stereotypes, which hinders the fullest acceptance and development of Chinese American women.

Although confronting with the racial discrimination in the new world, the Chinese decided to flee from calamitous China and earn fortune to survive in the turbulent days. Swarms of Chinese immigrants entered American when British defeated China in South China, forced terms of "Treaty of Nanjing", established "Treaty Ports" and ceded Hong Kong to Britain as a colony, by which China was forced to open its door to the West. Foreign presence in expanding array of "Treaty Ports", which included foreign concession such as urban districts under non-Chinese administration, grew rapidly. Moreover, the Taiping Revolution broke out in southern China from 1850–1864, against the ruling Manchu-led Qing Dynasty. It was the movement led by Hong Xiuquan, who announced that he had received visions in which he learned that he was the younger brother of Jesus. The rebel agenda included social reforms such as shared "property in common," equality for women, and the replacement of Confucianism, Buddhism and Chinese folk religion with their form of Christianity. The Qing government eventually crushed the rebellion with the aid of French and British forces. At least 20 million people died, mainly civilians, in one of the deadliest military conflicts in history. As a result, Chinese people at that time lived a hard life under domestic strife and foreign aggression, which left an indelible imprint on them. Accordingly, when labor was scarce and expensive in the United States, Chinese immigrants went there to earn their prosperity and survive in the turbulent days. However, the presence of Chinese as cheap laborers was vehemently opposed by the white workers and politicians.

Being accused of stealing the Whites' jobs, Chinese immigrants became the target of white mobs' riots and the scapegoats of politicians' racist propaganda, and were discriminated against, rejected and threatened with exclusion. Frequent violence against Chinese finally led to the promulgation of *the Chinese Exclusion Act* on May 8th, 1882, which suspended the immigration of Chinese laborers and prohibited the naturalization of Chinese Americans in the United States. Even the citizenship that some Chinese Americans had obtained could not exempt them from the political, occupational and cultural discrimination in the American mainstream society. According to *the Chinese Exclusion Act*, the Chinese immigrants in America could not bring their wives and sons over nor marry the white women in America, which led to Chinese immigrants' bachelor society directly.

In *Mrs. Spring Fragrance*, Sui Sin Far, in an anti-mainstream manner, maintained her stance to reveal that Chinese Americans have the same nature as the WASPs, which challenged the state-sanctioned stereotype of the Chinese. As Elizabeth Ammons notes: "To permit people other than straight white men to tell their own stories and tell them on their own terms constitutes a serious threat to fundamental, hegemonic, white male constructions of and rules about sex, race, gender, culture, order and disorder, and subservience and dominance in the United States." (Ammons, 1991)[31] As a result, the American mainstream repelled writers of other races whose works threatened their hegemonic discourse. However, Sui Sin Far adopted an anti-mainstream manner and maintained her position to reveal Chinese Americans so as to assert that Chinese Americans have the same nature as the WASPs, which subverted the state-sanctioned stereotyped Chinese. Her works forced

American nationals to observe and consider the world of Chinese immigrants in a fresh way so as to change these immigrants' state of being in exotic places.

In order to deconstruct the exclusive discrimination and eliminate racial binary oppositions, Sui Sin Far, from the humanity perspective, attracts the white readers to subvert their traditional prejudice against Chinese immigrants and concern the harmful result caused by the ethnocentrism and earns their sympathy and comprehension by focusing on the Chinese immigrants' physical and psychological injuries caused by the White superiority ideology, and exposing the unjust immigrant restrictions, discriminative laws and bureaucracy in "In the Land of the Free", one short story of her *Mrs. Spring Fragrance*, which delineates the struggle of a Chinese immigrant couple to retrieve their son from the American government.

First, with the background of *the Chinese Exclusion Act* in the brief narrative, Sui Sin Far elucidated the racial prejudices experienced by Chinese-Americans and recent Chinese immigrants to America, focusing on the detrimental effects wrought by this discrimination on these immigrant families. For a reunion with her husband, Hom Hing Lae Choo just reaches San Francisco from China with her "Little One", whom she has carefully nursed and raised with tenderness and affection and her husband has never a chance to see. However, the first moment that Hom Hing has set eyes on his son and just as he is first embracing his child, United States Customs officers remorselessly sunder the child from his parents, claiming "there is nothing in the papers that you have shown us — your wife's paper and your own — having any bearing upon the child" (Sui, 1995)[94]. They totally and intentionally disregard the clear connection demonstrated by the family and their desire to be together. The same case would never and forever happen to the white passengers.

Then, with description of the reactions of the Chinese couple whose son was grabbed by American customs officers, Sui Sin Far challenges the stereotyped Chinese immigrants in the thinking mode of exclusive discrimination and reconstructs new female and male images by exposing those Chinese immigrants have the same feelings, emotions and thoughts as the so-called superior race. Hom Hing and his wife are helpless in the face of practical problems because of their identity of Chinese immigrants. The only option is to wait. As a result, Mother is scared by the loss of her child and weathers out a sleepless night to return to Customs the next day to reclaim her child, as the officers promised that Hing and she could. However, her son is not returned. With the passage of time, the probability of reclaiming their son is quickly fading. When the young lawyer asked Hom Hing how his wife is, Hom Hing shook his head mournfully and replied:

> "She seems less every day. Her food she takes only when I bid her and her tears fall continually. She finds no pleasure in dress or flowers and cares not to see her friends. Her eyes stare all night. I think another moon she will pass into the land of spirits". (Sui, 1995)[98]

According to Hong Hing's response, the readers readily imagine that the loss of the only son has a huge pressure on both mother and father. Physically, the size of the mother seems less and less day by day because she misses and worries about her only child so much that she loses her natural instinct — appetite. Spiritually, she dissolves into tears every moment, ignores her makeup and friends, and weathers out every sleepless night. Mother deteriorates into a state that barely merits the title of life and will surely die if her child is not returned. Moreover, Hom Hing is helpless in this dilemma and is unable to do anything but suffer through the decline of his wife and the loss of his descendant. As a father, he is unable to protect his only son. As a husband, he is also unable to save his beloved wife, helplessly watching her dying little by little with bitter sadness. Both Hom Hing and his wife's reaction to the loss of their descendant is the same as the so-called superior race. The inferior race has the equivalent emotions and feelings as the white WASPs and they could be benevolent mother and sensitive father and husband, which subverts the other image created by American mainstream society.

Next, Sui Sin Far disintegrates the superiority by exposing the hypocrisy of the new world that advocates fraternity, liberty and equality by exposing that freedom is not free to the Chinese immigrants because of racial discrimination, and furthermore subverting the stereotyped images of barbarian and underdeveloped Chinese men and evil and uncivilized women in American mainstream literature. In a totally strange new environment, their two-year-old "Little One" is compelled to stay in a mission home and be kept apart from his own parents, although his father believes that "there cannot be any law that would keep a child from its mother" (Sui, 1995)[96]. Ironically, in this land of the free, there does exist such a ridiculous law that could rob people's freedom freely just according to their ethnicity. Freedom is not free in this land of the free. The little boy is only retrieved after Choo and Hing are essentially deprived of their family valuables by a cruelly opportunistic lawyer who squeezes their very last dime. When the wife knows that her husband has next to nothing left after he last paid the lawyer for writing letters and see the Custom officers, Lae Choo slips a heavy gold bracelet and holds it to the lawyer. When the lawyer refuses to accept it, Hong Ming told him: "It's all right, pure China gold. My wife's parent give it to her when we married." (Sui, 1995)[100] After Hom Hing's wife piles up all her jewels before the lawyer, Sui Sin Far details:

> "Hom Hing laid a restraining hand upon her shoulder. "Not all, my wife," he said in Chinese. He selected a ring — his gift to Lae Choo when she dreamed of the tree with the red flower. The rest of the jewels he pushed toward the white man." (Sui, 1995)[100]

According to this detail, readers easily know that Hom Hing is a sentimental husband who cherishes the precious moment with his wife in their life. Such a romantic Chinese man deconstructs, to some extent, the stereotypes of Chinese male characters in the previous literary writings. Accordingly, the lawyer's help is a pyrrhic victory: Choo sacrifices the possessions that define her heritage and familial tradition for the sake of the uncertain chance of reclaiming her son, transferring them to a man that cares little else for her possessions besides their monetary value. For her immense sacrifice she is not immediately returned the child she was pregnant for ten months and gave birth to. After ten months where "the sun had ceased to shine" for her, Choo is reunited with her Little One, whose only response upon perceiving the woman, who he used to know and love as his mother, is "go'way, go'way" (Sui, 1995)[101]. The last scene in the story is like a dagger that stabs the inner heart of the readers. After yearning day and night and staking all they have, what the pathetic mother gets from her beloved son is rejection. The institutionalized racism thinks nothing of separating parents from children. Thus, the so-called superior race exerts tremendous trauma on the inferior race. The so-called humane race relies on institutions to do inhumane things.

Furthermore, besides construction the humanity, sensitivity and civilization of the inferior race, Sui Sin Far deconstructs the humanity of the superior race by vehemently attacking the first act of discrimination at the Customs Office by the conversation between the insensitive customs officers:

> "'This little fellow,' said he, 'is visiting America for the first time.'
>
> The other custom officer stroked his chin reflectively.
>
> 'Good day,' said Hom Hing.
>
> 'Wait!' commanded one of the officers. 'You cannot go just yet.'
>
> 'What more now?' asked Hom Hing.
>
> 'I'm afraid,' said the first customs officer, 'that we cannot allow the boy to go ashore. There is nothing in the papers that you have shown us — your wife's papers and your own — having any bearing upon the child.'
>
> …
>
> The first officer turned to Hom Hing with an official tone of voice, said: 'seeing that the boy has no certificate entitling him to admission to this country, you will have to leave him with us'." (Sui, 1995)[93-94]

On the basis of the above conversation between the customs officers, readers know that although a white family would not even have been asked for documentation if they were coming through Customs, these officers are unwilling to let one child that is undoubtedly the son of Hom Hing and Lae Choo through Customs simply because their documents do not say that they have a child. In their official conversation, Hom Hing is of course a weak part. Furthermore, after Hom Hing explains them why his wife and son come back to China after twenty-moon time for the sake of his old dying parents, the officers are not moved but take away the two-year-old boy and give the family empty promises and, ultimately, leave them utterly hopeless in their struggle to retrieve their child. Sui Sin Far juxtaposes the so-called superior race without humanity and the so-called inferior race with humanity and thus queries who on earth is the superior race and who is the inferior one.

In order to deconstruct the superiority of the WASPs, Sui Sin Far attacks the death of humanity and intuitive knowledge caused by institutionalized racism by strongly assailing the lawyer, James Clancy in her narrative for his depredating the Chinese immigrant family's possessions because he feels it is okay to take advantage of Hom Hing and Lae Choo since they are Chinese immigrants. As Lae Choo says, he is just a "common white man" (Sui, 1995)[99]. The only thing he shows interest is money. In fact, James Clancy is the representative of the government. Despite doing different jobs, the customs officers and lawyer have the same ground, namely, they work for the government.

Sui Sin Far exposes that institutionalized racism possesses so influential leadership power on the mass multitudes that the government officials and lawyers inescapably exert the policy of racial discrimination into practice when they work for the government that implements institutionalized racism. The institutionalized racism, to some extent, suffocates their humanity and intuitive knowledge. According to James Madison, "government is the greatest of all reflections on human nature" (Madison, 1788)[51]. Thus, human nature is political. Human beings cannot live alone, and they all live in a society. Society is social, which consists of many layers. When the society is influential on human beings, they change, or rather, one part of their human nature changes. Just as Karl Marx argues, human beings can be influenced by environment. This is the socialization of human nature, which is changeable as the environment changes. Yet, there is another aspect of human nature, namely, the natural attribute of human nature. It is determined by genes, and everyone has it. The three officers' behaviors in the narrative are the reflection of their human nature which at that moment is never natural but political. As Thomas Hobbes argues, "human nature is political by political living under civil government" (Berry, 2006)[830]. The government officials inevitably put racial discrimination into practice when they work for the government that implements institutionalized racism. The institutionalized racism, to some extent, suffocates their humanity and intuitive knowledge. Far's poignancy is strongest in the closing scene, where she reveals the prodigious extent that the separating of child and mother had destroyed the family.

> "She fell on her knees and stretched her hungry arms toward her son.
> But the little One shrunk from her and tried to hide himself in the folds of the white woman's skirt.
> "Go'way, go'way!" he bade his mother." (Sui, 1995)[101]

When Mother kneels on the ground, waiting desirously for her son after enduring ten-month torture and undergoing all kinds of hardships, her beloved boy is unable to recognize his own mother and bid her to go away. The ten-month separating of child and mother sunders the strong family bonds of affection. Sui Sin Far pinpoints penetratingly that Chinese immigrants could expect severe discrimination in a society that professes freedom and equality for all. The disastrous consequences of institutionalized racism force the white readers realize that racial discrimination wreaked havoc on the humanity and then query the validity of *the Chinese Exclusion Act*. Thus, Sui Sin Far's stories conduce to awakening feelings of retrospection, empathy and sympathy in the White readers so that the consciousness of binary opposition of race could be deconstructed, to some extent.

Against the oriental view of that the East as the inferior Other and the West superiority, Sui Sin Far challenged the cultural hegemony of Western colonial discourse by explaining the reality and exposing universality of human nature in a Chinese couple and an interracial couple respectively in both *In the Land of the Free* and *The Story of One White Woman Who Married a Chinese*. Holding the view of “the whole world as one family” with the idea of universality of human nature as its core and one family as its form, Sui Sin Far attempts to reconstruct a utopian community by depicting the humanity of Chinese Americans and promoting ethnic integration and harmony between White Americans and Chinese Americans. The stereotyped oriental view establishes for the Westerners a sense of cultural and intellectual superiority and that the Easterners are constructed as inferior “Other”, different from them, reduced to silence and fetishised as an idol without the universal humanity. Deconstruction of the binary opposition in race and exposure of racial discrimination jeopardy are not Sui Sin Far’s ultimate goal because she wants to reconstruct a utopian world in America which is peopled with racial discrimination. Focusing on the humanity of human nature in the Chinese Americans and Chinese immigrants, Sui Sin Far subverts the stereotypes of Chinese people in American mainstream society.

Edward Said explores the Eurocentric view in the field of post-colonial theory in terms of subject/object, self/other in his pioneering work *Orientalism*. The Orient, according to Edward Said, is a “European invention,” a “place of romance, exotic beings, haunting memories and landscapes, remarkable experiences” (Said, 1979)[1]. Orientalism in Said’s view involves mainly three aspects. The first is that

Orientalism, claiming to be an objective academic scholarship, is more associated with politics in that it provides assistance for European and American expansion and colonization. The second is that Orientalism has helped Europeans and Americans to establish their self-image. The construction of identity in every age and every society, according to Said, involves the establishment of opposites and the "Other", because "the development and maintenance of every culture require the existence of another different and competing alter ego" (Said, 1995)[35]. The third is that Orientalism has produced a false description of Asian culture because the Westerners take an essentialised stance in their outlook. In other words, Orientalism regards Eastern culture as fixed and changeless, incapable of defining self. This stereotyped view establishes for the Westerners a sense of cultural and intellectual superiority. In Western intellectual discourse, the Easterners are constructed as "Other", different from them, reduced to silence and fetishised as an idol to be dominated. To the colonists, the construction of an "Other" is one thing and to make the other subject to this knowledge is another. Once deprived of the sense of identity and belonging, the individuals would become silent without resistance and become "individuals without an anchor, without horizon, colourless, rootless — a race of angels" (Fanon, 1968)[218]. It is because of this that "the people previously known as Orientals and now designated as Asian Americans have almost all, at one time or another, been excluded from U.S. citizenship" (Wong, 1993)[5].

Said's contribution to post-colonial studies lies in his critique of cultural hegemony of Western colonial discourse. According to Antonio Gramsci's ideas, the concept of hegemony is ideological domination. When one ideology, or world view, dominates, it suppresses or stamps out, often cruelly, any other ways of explaining reality. Actually, hegemony can contain a variety of ideologies. These consist of a culture's way of seeing and believing, and the institutions that uphold these beliefs, like religion, education, family, and the media. Through these beliefs and institutions, society endorses the ethical beliefs and manners which "the powers that be" agree are true, or right, or logical, or moral. The institutions and beliefs that the dominant culture supports are so powerful, and get hold of people when they are so young, that alternative ways of envisioning reality are very hard to imagine. This is how hegemony is created and maintained. It calls attention to "political and material effects of Western scholarship and academic institutions" by revealing the West's hegemony over the East in "producing the East discursively as the West's inferior Other and strengthens West's self-image of superiority" (Moore-Gilbert, 1997)[36]. What Said emphasizes is the binary opposition between the colonizer and the colonized.

Subverting the inferior East Other and the West Self, Sui Sin Far challenges the cultural hegemony of Western colonial discourse by explaining the reality and exposing universality of human nature in a Chinese couple and an interracial couple respectively in both *In the Land of the Free* and *The Story of One White Woman Who Married a Chinese*, respectively. On the one hand, in order to reconstruct a utopian world with the idea of universality of human nature as its core, Sui Sin Far moulds the protagonist of Lae Choo as a mother with the universal features of a common paterfamilias by displaying her mental self-torture and material sacrifice for the sake of reclaiming her son. Ever since her little son is robbed at the Customs on the first day they arrived in San Francisco, the Chinese mother is sad and unfree mentally, and her daily life in the new land is miserable. She sheds tears and cannot sleep well because her mind is engrossed wholly with the idea of how to make her child come back. "The winter rains were over: the spring had come to California, flushing the hills with green and causing an ever-changing pageant of flowers to pass over them. But there was no spring in Lae Choo's heart, for the Little One remained away from her arms." (Sui, 1995)[97] In the spring which symbolizes life and a new start in a cycle, Lae Choo has born intense moral suffering for many days, experiencing her hardest time as a mother who lost her only child. She sacrifices the possessions that represent her heritage and familial tradition in order to get her child back. Thus, Sui Sin Far's depiction of Lae Choo manifests the glorious beauty of maternal nature.

On the other hand, besides molding a universal mother image, Sui Sin Far shapes Hom Hing as a responsible and affectionate father and husband with the universality of human nature, which is the other gender in a utopian world. The responsible husband concerns about and worries about his wife. "If the boy not come home I lose my wife sure, continued Hom Hing with bitter sadness." (Sui, 1995)[98] Moreover, although the husband is free in act because he has the certificate which makes him move freely in California, his mind is confined because the only thing he really cares about is his family — his child and his wife. According to Sui Sin Far's minute description of Hom Hing's reaction to the crack-up of his wife, a responsible husband with sensitivity stands vividly on the paper. Thus, the figure of the husband subverts such stereotypes of Chinese men as criminals, gamblers, sly thugs, and opium smoker created by the White writers in the American mainstream literature.

In order to reconstruct a utopian world, Sui Sin Far highlighted the equality and harmony among different ethnicities, portrayed the universality of Chinese human nature, and subverted the stereotypes in American mainstream. The couple's love for their child makes them do everything for the child's sake. According to Karl Marx, it is the basic instinct for human beings, such as love, hatred, worry, happiness and so on. It is a state of nature, which refers to philosophical assertions regarding the condition of human before social factors are imposed, thus attempting to describe the "natural essence" of human nature. The Chinese couple with the universality of human nature is in sharp contrast to the most pachydermatous and insensitive stereotype in the American mainstream media.

Holding "the whole world as one family" view, Sui Sin Far planned to promote ethnic integration and harmony between White Americans and minor ethnic groups, especially Chinese Americans. She adopted two indirect ways to reconstruct utopian community. One is through the protest and the other is by self-affirmation by the perspective of a white woman. Without influence of the thinking mode of exclusive discrimination based on the binary opposition in race, ethnicity, to a certain extent, could be integrated because different types of ethnicities are not mutually exclusive. Ethnic integration is able to ensure a balanced ethnic mix among various ethnic groups throughout the world.

Americans' prejudice and racial discrimination made no allowances of interracial marriage. As a result, interracial marriage is illegal and prevented by American laws before the 1967 Supreme Court decision. One of anti-miscegenation laws is *the Cable Act* passed in 1922, which formulates an idea that any female U.S. citizen will lose her citizenship if she marries a Chinese because Chinese are considered to be too dangerous to marry. In order to maintain Americans' purity and power, Americans do not marry Chinese and Chinese are not allowed to marry Americans either. As Annette White-Parks argues in the foreword of her work *Sui Sin Far/Edith Maude Eaton: A Literary Biography*, "Sui Sin Far's work speared in what was for Asians, the era of exclusion, when Chinese and other Asians in North America were at the very bottom of the ethno-cultural pyramid, with a legal status lower than that of African Americans or African Canadian" (White-Parks, 1995) [xi].

In such a very severe case, Sui Sin Far attempted to reconstruct a utopian family by protesting the American authoritative act, self-affirming the humane merits of Chinese Americans, exploring the sensitive issue of interracial marriage in her short stories. She showed how interracial love and marriage are not only possible but also fulfilling if the racial discrimination and prejudice could be eliminated. Thus, she sketched the contour of an embryonic form of a utopian world with one family as its form. *The Story of One White Woman Who Married a Chinese* relates a story of a Caucasian woman who is abandoned by her abusive white husband and marries a Chinese man. The story portrays a Caucasian American Minnie, who takes her six-year-old child and leaves her American husband who has betrayed her. After the divorce is finalized, Minnie finds herself on the brink of destruction. On the verge of committing suicide, Minnie is saved by, befriended by, and soon marries, a Chinese businessman with the name of Liu Kanghi. In contrast to her former husband, her Chinese husband is kind, generous, and backup. Their marriage is, to some extent, blissful, and they live harmoniously in the Chinese American community. Together, they raise the children from her previous marriage with the children conceived of their marriage although Minnie has to face many outside prejudices and doubts. Through these characters, Sui Sin Far shows how interracial love and marriage are not only possible but also fulfilling if the racial discrimination act could be annihilated.

Sui Sin Far protested the American authoritative act and affirmed the humane merits of Chinese Americans in *The Story of One White Woman Who Married a Chinese* by revolving around two emotions — love and hostility. Through the Caucasian American woman's eyes, Sui Sin Far explored emotional aspects of two kinds of ethnicities by depicting the relationship between husband and wife.

Emotions of attachment take time to develop, and that is why people often say love does not come cheap. Moreover, Spinoza says: "The human being is a miraculous creature, and his miracle consists in his capacity for love. But it is just here that the tragic difficulty arises. For man must realize that his capacity for love gives him no right to demand that anyone love him in return." (Margolis, 1998)[148] Just as Spinoza's statement, when our expectation of love is attained, love is considered to be enjoyable; when not, we shall feel hurt. Whoever lacks sufficient rationality in their mind would use withdrawal, denial and other forms of avoidance to deal with their hurts. Then, the avoidance of hurts can lead to the avoidance of intimacy. According to R. W. Leeper, "emotions give behavior (and mental activity) its goal-directedness, allowing us to choose between alternatives" (Strongman, 1996)[84]. Hence, if a self succeeds to make the right decision in the choice of certain alternatives for solving the emotional dilemma, desirable consequences might be resulted to the self. *The Story of One White Woman Who Married a Chinese* boasts sufficient proof for this point. In the opening of the story, Sui Sin Far enumerated three reasons for Minnie to marry a Chinese instead of a white American.

> "Well, in the first place, because I loved him; in the second place, because I was weary of working, struggling and fighting with the world; in the third place, because my child needed a home." (Sui, 1995)[66-67]

The three reasons announce Minnie's determination to marry a Chinese American who has been reared to prejudice against. The young Chinese merchant Liu Kanghi saves Minnie when she is grimly determined to drown herself and her baby after being rejected by her white husband. Without his assistance, both Minnie and her six-year-old child would be doomed to pass away in their blooming years. Besides preventing her body from jaws of the death, Liu renders her selfishless spirit concern and help so that Minnie obtains the desire to live on. Liu also raises Minnie's child from her first husband. Moreover, the avoidance of hurts from her former husband naturally makes Minnie choose between alternatives. So, as a woman and mother, Minnie inevitably falls in love with Liu Kanghi who offers her everything as a husband and father. Without regard to his ethnicity, he is a perfect husband and father. Thus, Sui Sin Far sketches the contour of the foundation of one family — mutual love and support.

After living with Chinese Americans for some time, Minnie realized: "My life's experience had taught me that the virtues do not always belong to the whites. I was interested in all that concerned the Liu household, became acquainted with all their friends, and lost altogether the prejudice against the foreigner in which I had been reared." (Sui, 1995)[74] After living with a Chinese family, Minnie gradually rejects the prejudices and blends in with this big family. Furthermore, Sui Sin Far compares Minnie's former white husband James with the Chinese merchant Liu Kanghi from the perspective of Minnie after she was threatened by ex-husband:

> "… Yes, honorably and like a man. And what are you that dare sneer at one like him. For all your six feet of grossness, your small soul cannot measure up to his great one. You were unwilling to protect and care for the woman who was your wife or the little child you caused to dome into this world; but he succored and saved the stranger woman, treated her as a woman, with reverence and respect; gave her child a home, and made them both independent, not only of others but of himself." (Sui, 1995)[76-77]

The comparison between the American white man and the Chinese merchant highlights Chinese virtues. Minnie's happy experience in the interracial marriage exposes that love link different ethnical groups into one family.

The successful and harmonious union of the white woman and the Chinese man indicates that people from different ethnicities could live blissfully in one family and could live harmoniously in one society. There is no superiority or inferiority in different ethnicities, but only differences. Only if the Whites regard the non-Whites as themselves and the Whites have no racial prejudice and discrimination toward the non-Whites, can different ethnic groups live together peacefully and properly in a utopian community.

Sui Sin Far believed that there was no essential difference between Chinese Americans and people in other nations, and called for the harmony of different nations, just as what she wrote in *Leaves from the Mental Portfolio of a Eurasian*:

> "Fundamentally, all people are the same. My mother's race is as prejudiced as my father's. Only when the whole world becomes as one family will human beings be able to see clearly and distinctly." (Sui, 1995)[129]

As a Eurasian writer, Sui Sin Far not only had insight into the issue of racism of her age, but also devoted herself to the fighting against racial discriminations with her works, advocating the establishment of a utopian community where people of all races throughout the world could live harmoniously.

Probing deeply into Chinatown and its inhabitants' lives, she successfully created a more objective image of Chinese Americans that American mainstream writers ignored and distorted through the ages. Over one hundred years, stereotyped names such as Chinks, John Chinaman, and Yellow Peril have been imposed upon Chinese immigrants in various literary and historical works. Although the names might vary according to the changes in the nature and degree of prejudice against Chinese immigrants, the unfriendliness and distance remained the same. Although some people advised Sui Sin Far to play the role of a curio peddler and sell exotic Chinese culture, she had no intention of appealing to the curiosity of the reading public. What she did in her life was to record the ethnic experience of Chinese Americans and draw an original and realistic picture for them by dipping into the deeper currents beneath the surface of Chinatown and the lives of its inhabitants. Owing to her talent and deep insight, Sui created a more objective image of Chinese Americans so successfully that she deconstructed the negative stereotypes of Chinese Americans in American mainstream literature and reconstruct a utopian world with one family as its core. Yin Xiaohuang was impressed by Sui Sin Far's achievement of breaking the stereotype of Chinese Americans in popular literature at that time:

> "Miss Eaton has struck a new note in American fiction. The thing she has tried to do is to portray for readers of the white race the lives, feelings, sentiments of the Americanized Chinese of the Pacific Coast, of those who have intermarried with them and of the children who have sprung from such unions." (Yin, 2000)[91]

In *Mrs. Spring Fragrance and Other Writings*, Sui Sin Far expresses both her feelings as a Eurasian and her keen desire to tell what kind of people Chinese Americans were in a time of strong literary bias against writers of Chinese ancestry and makes it possible to correct mistaken images in common Americans' minds with her talent and deep insight. Thus, Sui Sin Far conceives of an imaginary utopian world with the idea of "universality of human nature" as its core and one family as its form.

In conclusion, Sui Sin Far's writing deconstructs racial stereotypes and displays the absolute difference between imaginary characters in Orientalism and the real Chinese immigrants so as to challenge the western cultural hegemony. Just as Diana Vanessa Holford states in *Biracial/Bicultural Identity in the Writings of Sui Sin Far*, by addressing the artistic and psychological complexity of Sui Sin Far's treatment of the biracial character and of interracial marriage, Sui Sin Far deconstructs Orientalism by dramatizing the deconstructive ways in which North American culture defines the Chinese as inhuman "other" in order to prevent interracial understanding and maintain profitable power structures (Holford, 2001)[161].

3.2 Deconstruction of American Dreams in *East Goes West*

Unlike his peers who mainly concentrate the Korean memory, Younghill Kang, as the only and first Korean immigrant to write novels in English in the first-generation Korean American writers by 1965, describes his immigrant experiences in the U.S. The general characteristic in most works written by the first-generation Korean immigrant writers who came to U.S. by 1965 focuses not on immigrant life but on memories of Korea because they confront double influences of U.S. racial discrimination and Japan's colonization. Moreover, unlike the Chinese, the Koreans lacked an economic foundation for ethnic solidarity, but they felt a strong sense of ethnicity which was even more intense than the Chinese, and had source for community: powered by a unique necessity of struggling against Japanese colonialism in Korea. Thus, the strong sense of nationalism is revealed in their literature. Most of Korean immigrant writers of the first generation demonstrate the Korean nationalism in their literature. However, Younghill Kang concentrates more on the new life of Korean Americans on the host land.

Like Chinese American literature, members of an elite class of educated immigrants uttered the early voice of Korean American literature largely in the form of autobiography. The best known of these early writers is Yonghill Kang (1903–1972), a precursor of Korean American writing and the father of Korean American literature. He was born in Hamgyeong-do in northern Korea and educated at first in the Chinese Confucian tradition and later at Western Christian Schools which were established all over Korea by missionaries from North America. He belonged to the Korean upper-class and thus was educated and well-read in the Chinese classics as well as in the western literature. He reached the United States in 1921 before the enactment of laws that excluded Korean immigrants for more than thirty years. He attended classes at Harvard and Boston Universities and read English and American classics voraciously while working at various jobs to support himself. He began writing in English with the help of his American wife, Frances Keeley. In *Asian American Literature: An Introduction to the Writings and Their Social Context,* Elaine H. Kim once wrote about Younghill Kang: "Kang was a unique figure for his time, the only Korean immigrant to have written book-length fiction in English, and autobiographical fiction at that. In this and in many other ways he was completely unrepresentative of his people, yet became something of a spokesman for Koreans in America almost by default." (Kim, 2006)[33]

As the first and the best known of the early Korean American novelists, Younghill Kang wrote two interconnected autobiographical novels. *The Grass Roof* was published in 1931 and *East Goes West* in 1937. While the former depicts the life of the personal narrator in Korea, the latter describes his experiences in the U.S. As the first Korean American to write novels, although with an autobiographical touch, Younghill Kang represented Korea and Koreans to Western readers, for whom he was both importer of the unfamiliar, in terms of a remote Oriental nation, and reinforcer of the familiar, in terms of popular notions about backward peoples craving for the American dream.

Although Younghill Kang considered *East Goes West* "more mature in style and technique" as well as "more highly developed in content", it was *The Grass Roof* won him accolades in America and Europe. In *An Interethnic Companion to Asian American Literature*, Elaine H. Kim writes: "He is said to have commented that it was his great misfortune that Pearl buck's Pulitzer Prize-winning novel about China, *The Good Earth*, was published in the same year as *The Grass Roof,* eclipsing his own Asian tale." (Kim, 1997)[183] The book has its popularity in part because of its novelty: it took place in Korea of which very little was known in the west.

As the companion volume of *East Goes West*, *The Grass Roof* is an apologia for the protagonist Chung-pa Han's breathless departure from Korea so it is less about his father land of Korea than about Chung-pa Han's desire and eagerness for the West. Unlike his peers, Chung-pa Han does not participate in the movement for national liberation from Japanese occupation during the bitter years just prior to his departure for the U.S. in 1921. His brief imprisonment by the Japanese after his peripheral participation in the widespread March First Independence Movement in 1919 only reinforces his desire to escape from the country. Chung-pa Han decides against mass movements and narrow nationalism for the sake of individual survival. The Universal truths inspired by his readings of Shakespeare and western philosophy reinforce his desire to flee from Korea. Disappointed by the traditional education as well as by Japanese schooling in Korea, he concludes that life in Korea is too restrictive for an energetic searcher like himself and that the real knowledge is attainable only outside Korea, in the West. Moreover, the Japanese conquest has changed his country from a small, provincial, old-fashioned Confucian nation into a planet of death. The only way to survive from the dead planet is to get away from his native land and go straight towards the western civilization. Thus, he escaped from the ancient spiritual planet that had been his father's home and has become a wasteland unable to sustain its youthful vitality. He is attracted as if by natural gravity toward the more important cultures of the West. He is, like Faustus, the protagonist of *The Tragical History of Doctor Faustus* by Christopher Marlowe, a lonely pioneer in a brave new world which, in his eyes, stands for the future, the new and the young while his beloved Korea represents an old and dying culture.

Absorbed by his desire to find his position in American society, Chung-pa Han endeavors to ignore his Korean past, his Korean identity and his Korean compatriots because he thinks most of them are stuck in the past, nostalgic for their homeland and reluctant to accept the new circumstances in the new land. But unfortunately, the American dream of individual freedom is not extended to marginalized immigrants from Asia, so Chung-pa Han finds himself pinned to remain within the borders of Chinatown with other Korean exiles. Although he was ever a rebellious individualist, he is different from his compatriots in that he cannot accept the revolutionary fervor of fellow Koreans who are obsessed by their desire to return one day in their life to a liberated native land. Although they remain exiled in body in the alien land, these most typical Koreans often donate their hard-earned money to the independence movement in Korean revolution against Japan, have an ambition to return Korea, settle down and raise 100 percent Korean children who would be just as patriotic as themselves. The idea of returning to Korea never attracts him: "If I went back to Korea, and I returned to become a villager as always, was that any fun? Why should I keep on manufacturing babies for which there would be no future?" (Kang, 1931)[259] As a result, lacking their nationalist passion, Chung-pa Han feels loneliness and a sense of alienation even among his fellow countrymen because unlike them, he is eager to escape the ruin and decaying land to come to the Promised Land that is peopled with creative promises.

Instead of taking readers on an immigrant's journey from a penniless immigrant to a successful citizen, Younghill Kang deconstructs the mottos of progress, equality, assimilation and upward mobility advocated by American dream by his four major Korean immigrants who fail to achieve their American dreams in *East Goes West*. By intersecting Emersonian American dream and Franklinian American dream through the characters, Younghill Kang reveals that both a material Utopia and a moral Utopia are daydreams for the marginal Korean immigrants. Their process of pursuing material value and spiritual harbor gradually evolves a heartbreaking nightmare. They want to be a part of the U.S., yet they are apart by the very U.S. that advocates beliefs in the unity of the family, the healthiness of competition in society, the need for success and money on a low level and emphasizes that the new self should be a moral self, with its duty of always becoming, always extending and newly uttering the possibilities of life.

East Goes West presents an unflattering opinion of the underside of American life from the perspectives of people prohibited by the color bar by concerning their work, their aspirations and the exclusion from American social and intellectual life. Younghill Kang himself thought that *East Goes West* "more mature in style and technique" as well as "more highly developed in content" than the first: "*The Grass Roof* may be said to have been written in the mood of the Everlasting Nay of Carlyle; *East Goes West* may be compared to the mood of the everlasting Yea." (Kunitz, 1955)[744] While his first novel mainly depicts Chung-pa Han's life in Korea before he emigrated to the west, the second is a depiction about the lives of the Korean exiled immigrants who are living in the urban America during the 1920s and 1930s and are the invisible to U.S. American readers.

Harboring and adoring the American dream which stands for the promising future and the new start, the Korean exiled immigrants soon realize, however, that there is a discrepancy between the west they know from literature and the west they themselves experience. With the depiction of Korean immigrants' endless wandering, the writer questions the American nationalist narrative of progress, equality, assimilation and upward mobility, which, to some extent, is a kind of American dream for those immigrants from other parts of the world to quest. Elaine H. Kim once pointed out that Younghill Kang saw himself not as a guest or visitor to the United States but sincerely tried to find a place for himself in the country and to make, at a very early point in his life, the transition from Korean to Korean American (Berner, 2003)[109]. Although he was the person who wanted to be assimilated into the American society, Younghill Kang found he was apart by the very U.S. as a colored people who should have the self-knowledge that these glaring American dreams are not for them because they are in a de-privileging position. In his second autobiographical fiction, Younghill Kang creates four characters of Mr. Pak, George Jum, Chung-pa Han and To Wan Kim who endeavor to find room in the

United States in their various ways, which indicates that Younghill Kang indeed attempts to find a place in the new land in a proper way.

Actually, what attracts those Korean immigrants is the two American dreams. Unlike the Chinese immigrants of the first generation, the Korean immigrants of the first generation were confronted with double oppressions of U.S. racial discrimination and Japan's occupation, which meant that the first generation of Korean immigrants in the U.S. was totally marooned. In a condition of utter helplessness, they were unable to have recourse to their native land which was colonized by Japan. Moreover, unlike the Chinese on the mainland, the Koreans lacked an economic foundation for ethnic solidarity, but they felt a strong sense of ethnicity which was even more intense than the Chinese, and had source for community: powered by a unique necessity of struggling against Japanese colonialism in Korea. As a result, the motto of progress, equality, assimilation and upward mobility advocated by American dream appealed to the Koreans who wanted to find their spiritual peace in the mental utopia and wealth in the material utopia. One American dream is represented by Benjamin Franklin, the original representative of American dream, which is actually a kind of material value that thousands of American common mass multitudes pursue at all costs. The other dream is embodied by Ralph Waldo Emerson, the radical representative of American dream, which is one of spiritual ideals perceived as a promise of prosperity for its people. In the novel, the author attempts to intersect the two American dreams through the characters.

As an American essayist, lecturer and poet, who led the transcendentalist movement of the mid-19th century, Ralph Waldo Emerson represents the American spiritual and moral dream. Compared with Franklinian American dream, a kind of materialism that is ignorant of the inner and positive meaning of the freedom and is unconscious of the case of positive moral values or genuinely spiritual perspectives of human life, Emersonian interpretation of American dream is an exploration of freedom, whose nature, consequence and effect on human life are the concentration. Emerson scrutinizes American dream from a moral and spiritual perspective, which stands on a higher level than Benjamin Franklin's version. For Emerson self-reliance is built on trust, but it was not a trust in the ordinary self of the economic marketplace. Self-reliance starts with a dependence on God and experiences the process of a purgation of the ordinary self. Namely, the ordinary self, the self at the level of Franklinian materialism, develops a dependence on God. Under the power of the belief, it is sublimed from the material level to the spiritual one step by step. Finally, a brand-new self, the Emersonian self comes into being. As a matter of fact, the nature of Emerson's self is the emphasis on morality or codes of ethics deriving from Puritanism, which not only contradicts to Franklin's self based on wealth but also offers a way of salvation that redeems people from Franklin's excessively materialized dream. Emerson's American dream manifests people a moral Garden of Eden and a promising future, which is a moral challenge to the material world. Emerson's moral concern apparently arouses more acclaims and acknowledgements from the common multitude because he revalues the meaning of the American experience, and emphasizes that the new self should be a moral self, with its duty of always becoming, always extending and newly uttering the possibilities of life. The conflict between the two American dreams finds itself fully and dramatically in *East Goes West*. One dream is to achieve material attainments like wealth and leisure, while the other is to seek a spiritual harbor. Through the dramatized conflicts, the four characters fail to achieve their American dreams.

With the portrayal of the sundry male characters in *East Goes West*, Younghill Kang intertwined and deconstructed two kinds of American dreams — Emersonian and Franklinian dreams which represent a mental utopia and a material utopia, respectively. *East Goes West* is the miserable record of Chung-pa Han's unsuccessful search for his Emersonian American dream of his imagination — a mental utopia which is a place of regeneration, a glorious version of fascination and romance, and a secular format of a spiritual home. Chung-pa Han yearns for America for he believes that "you can think anything, see anything, learn anything" in America (Kang, 1937)[165]. After he noticed bitterly the miserable condition of his father land which had become a wasteland that had no warmth, that was under an infernal twilight, Chung-pa Han was grimly determined that he would hurtle forward to foreign body where "a younger culture" drew him "by natural gravity" (Kang, 1937)[4]. He hoped that he "entered a new life like one born again" and "wandered on soil as strange as Mars, seeking roots, roots for an exile's soul" (Kang, 1937)[5]. Determined to quest for his Emersonian American dream — his mental utopia, Chung-pa Han set off from the old walled Korean city some thousand years old — Seoul — famous for poets and scholars to New York. It was in New York he felt he was destined really to come out from the boat. In Korea to come out from the boat is an idiom meaning to be born, as the word "pai" for "womb" is the same as "pai" for "boat". The beginning of his new existence started to be founded in the new land.

From his protagonist Chung-pa Han's acknowledgement, Younghill Kang demonstrated his American dream — building a bridge from the secular world into a mental utopia. At the very beginning of the novel, Younghill Kang constructs his protagonist's Emersonian American dream-seeking an opening into American life through scholarship and study in order to seek out a secular format of a mental utopia. With his American dream of becoming "educated like J.P. Ok, B.D., M.S.T., M.A., Ph.D.", Chung-pa Han attends night school college classes, hoping to find unifying principles he is looking for (Kang, 1937)[57]. In the end, after he endures lots of trials and tribulations, he fails, admitting that "I could build no bridge from one classroom to another, just as I could build no bridge from the New Hotel (where he works as a kitchen helper) into the mental Utopia" (Kang, 1937)[203]. Thus, his faith in books as the key to the West seems too ideal and hapless. What Chung-pa Han wants to acquire through the kingdom of bookworms has become so bleak that he could only turn inward to search for the lost Utopia through his imagination:

> "Thank God here were nights, long lonely hours to think, to become me again, to try to recapture the magic and mystery with which I had first dreamed America. I could find it no longer in books, the books I had brought from college…, though I read again and again." (Kang, 1937)[328]

Once he could gain spiritual gratifications by swimming into the depths of Browning's spiritual sea, resting himself under Tennysonian sunsets, diving in through frothy Swinburnian waves, sitting on the Rossetti borderland of the seen bank and the unseen yonder horizon, meditating in Arnold's academic cloister and finding relaxation in Morris' earthy paradise and utopian vision. Thus, Younghill Kang makes Chung-pa Han construct his Emersonian American dream by having learned about the West world through struggling to read Chaucer, Shakespeare, Romantic poetry, and Victorian prose.

Younghill Kang deconstructs Chung-pa Han's Emersonian American dream by his failure to quest it. In the process of pursuing his mental utopia, Chung-pa Han is exploited, ridiculed, despised, mistreated, and utilized by various employers and whites. Chung-pa Han's failure to fulfill his dream comes from his experiences at the margins of the U.S. though he constructs his spiritual utopia through the mainstream western classics. When he interacts with paternalistic missionaries, avaricious businessmen, and haughty politicians, or when he works as a house servant, kitchen helper, farm hand, peddler, and department store clerk, Chung-pa Han confronts the sundry troubles and problems that the books he read are unable to give a reply. He is desperate to find that:

> "... somehow I could not recite Thomas Carlyle and John Ruskin with quite the old satisfaction in my drab little room... 'Work, work, work, there is a perennial nobleness, even sacredness in work... . Blessed is he who has found his work let him ask no other blessedness...' How did that fir in with selling cherry-wood stands? As for Ruskin, 'Magnanimous, magnanimous, magnanimous is life'... I had always liked that adjective, magnanimous, but Ruskin now sickened me... I read once more about Maude and Madelaine, then threw the book from one end of the room to the other. Even Browning was English fog in the lungs..." (Kang, 1937)[328-329]

The above desperate soliloquy derives from his miserable personal experience in the U.S. when he pursues his Emersonian American dream. Having been refused a job at the Harlem YMCA, which is reserved only for whites, he sleeps in nickel flophouses and mingles with the bums there and roves with the Korean exiles in New York

Chinatown. Then he has the chance to work as a domestic servant for a white family who mistreats him like a cat or dog. After that he finds a job as a busboy in a Chinese restaurant, where Asian waiters with PhDs and medical degrees serve the white prostitutes and petty criminals. He vends tea from place to place in Harlem, where he and his fellow Koreans are not abused as they are by the whites with steely eyes and superior shrewdness uptown. Even though a missionary scholarship offers him the chance to jumble with non-Asians in a small theological college in British Columbia and he seizes the opportunity, his experiences on the campus only reinforce his estrangement and alienation. While pursuing the Emersonian American dream, Chung-pa Han experiences various plights of being exploited, derided, contemned and abused from various employers and whites. At last, when he works as a clerk in the fake Oriental goods section of department store, he overhears racist remarks and sees salespeople compete inexorably with each other over pennies. Bit by bit, Younghill Kang deconstructs his protagonist's Emersonian American dream until Chung-pa Han comes to view the department store as a microcosm of the world and fully perceive the secret of American life:

> "This is American life… All day long the moving multitudes of humanity, with busy legs, constantly darting false smiles to cover their depressed facial expression, the worn-out machine bodies turning round in the aisles… two eyes to look at the customer, two hands to count the change… then to make a sale check, to carry the goods to the packing room, then to run with legs' tottering strength after a new customer, for fear of losing that sale to anther salesman, at last the dead-tired body moving from the cloak-room to breathe the air — the street air, the dusty,

> respectable, stale air of staid Philadelphia. But where were all the enchantment and romance, the glorious vision, which I had seen in my dreams of America as a boy?" (Kang, 1937)[318]

Keenly perceptive and highly sensitive to the apparently new and exciting world around him, Chung-pa Han finds out the secret core of the world in his dream — hypocrisy, covetousness and desperation without enchantment and romance he expected before. Astonished and disappointed by white ignorance and racism he encounters at every turn, he cannot understand why his hopes and desires never seem to match the reality that he confronts with year after discouraging year.

Despite the sad examples of his fellow exiles, Chung-pa Han is sure that he can succeed where they failed. But hunger starts early to interfere with his attempts to study the ideal of western civilization in his lonely and cold room: "In utter solitude and with a chilling heart, I feared pavement famine with plenty all around but in the end not even grass to chew… it was hard to concentrate. Even in the midst of Hamlet's subtlest soliloquies, I could think of nothing but food." (Kang, 1937)[32-33] There remains one possibility for Chung-pa Han to belong to America through an American girl. Influenced by To Wan Kim's romance with an American girl, he attempts to form an association with an American woman. He is so attracted with the idea of Western romantic love that he considers if he participates in it, even unrequited, he will become one part of western civilization. No matter efforts he makes, the American girl has no intention of befriending Chung-pa Han. His love for her is like his dream of America, only a hopeful fantasy.

After his failure of attempts to integrate into the United States through scholarship and study as well as an association with an American woman, Chung-pa

Han realized that his daydream of belonging in America is doomed to be shattered. Where there is progress, there is slavery, starvation, racial discrimination and no soul. Leaving Korea for America, Chung-pa Han is anxious to find a way to make of himself a bridge between developing East and developed West. He depicts his "purpose in coming to the West":

> "More and more I intellectualized my instinctive purpose in coming to the West. On my own cultural heritage, I wanted to ingraft the… Renaissance, to make from that something different, something new… my own rebirth. Thus, in approaching the West I was eager to feel its life in an unbroken stream pass though by hear-blood… Homer, Aeschylus, Christ, Augustine, Dante, Chaucer, Shakespeare… linked in continuous process of… life with its vast onward momentum… I wanted the whole Western hemisphere in one block." (Kang, 1937)[204]

According to the exposure of Chung-pa Han's instinctive purpose, readers readily know that the aim of the writer is to graft the best essence in the Western culture to the old East and advocate the integration of the East and West to create a mental utopia. However, in the end, Chung-pa Han is unsuccessful to make himself into a bridge that could communicate barriers between the East and the West. He remains an outsider because he is not granted access to American society. Like Cervantes's Don Quixote, Chung-pa Han sets forth to battle windmills throughout the American landscape, never ceasing to be deflated by the racial discrimination he encounters. He meets a chapter of disappointment, misunderstanding, loneliness and alienation which forces Chung-pa Han to reject his daydream of melting into the United States and accept the irreconcilable worlds of actuality and desire. Like Fitzgerald's great Gatsby, Chung-pa Han's Emersonian American dream dies through his picaresque adventures which expose the shallow materialism, hypocrisy, philistinism and inhumanity of life in capitalist America. With Chung-pa Han's failure to find an entry into American life, contradictions between the promise of freedom and the reality of racial discrimination, between economic survival and dreams of intellectual accomplishment, and between the ideal of America and actual experience of life in its margins still remain although Chung-pa Han clings to his naive faith in America's shining promise.

The novel ends with a significant dream, in which Chung-pa Han is struggling toward a dangerous suspension bridge to reach his childhood friends and a "paradise of wild and flowery magic" on the other side when he suddenly drops his money and car keys. Scrambling after them, he is beset by a dark cellar only to find himself trapped in with "some frightened-looking Negroes" and some red-faced white men are to set them all on fire. Both Franklinian and Emersonian dreams having failed him, Chung-pa Han turns to Asia for the answer:

> "I have remembered this dream, because, according to Oriental interpretation, it is a dream of good omen. To be killed in a dream means success and in particular death by fire augurs good fortune. This is supposed to be so, because death symbolizes I Buddhistic philosophy, growth and rebirth and a happier reincarnation." (Kang, 1937)[401]

Disillusionment of the American dreams ultimately forces the protagonist to retreat to a Buddhist interpretation of the dream — that he will be reincarnated to a better life. In the end, Chung-pa Han fails to find an entry into American life. Younghill Kang deconstructs Chung-pa Han's spiritual Garden of Eden by keeping the contradictions between the promise of freedom and the reality of race discrimination, between economic survival and dreams of intellectual accomplishment, and between the ideal of America and actual experience of life in its margin's existence. Thus, Younghill Kang succeeds in deconstructing his protagonist's Emersonian American dream. Chung-pa Han became disillusioned about his mental utopia at last after experiencing countless struggles and numerous intentional efforts.

The Franklinian American dream is a sequence of beliefs in the unity of the family, the need for success, the quest for freedom and equality and acquirement of material possessions, all of which derives from a kind of material value that sundry American mass multitudes pursue at all costs. Benjamin Franklin with working class roots, one of the founding fathers of the United States, embodied the American success dream in his *Autobiography* as well as in his real-life attainments. Franklin deems that a man has to obtain a certain amount of necessary property so that his fate will be controlled by himself and not by his creditors. The implicit indication in his *Autobiography* is that no man is free without money. Namely, the symbol of freedom is wealth which is not only the means but the end. To some extent, the Franklinian dream is a kind of materialism that is ignorant of the inner and positive meaning of the freedom and is unconscious of the case of positive moral values or genuinely spiritual perspectives of human life. For Benjamin Franklin, self-reliance is a dependence on one's self as an accumulator of wealth, that is, self-reliance is a necessary channel to become free from the power of money, from the poor to the rich, from the low class to the upper class. Its self is a satisfied self that does not doubt any deeper meaning of life. As a result, the Franklinian dream with reference to money could only lead to the disillusionment of the real dream and the real life finally, which is the least attractive form in his American dream because after people obtain the wealth, they have no goal of life, no spiritual sustenance, ultimately leading to lack of the sublimation of the inner world. F. Soctt Fitzgerald's great Gatsby is a proper case of the Franklinian dream.

Younghill Kang deconstructs the Franklinian American dream, a material utopia by the four characters of Mr. Pak, George Jum, Chung-pa Han and To Wan Kim who endeavor and fail to find room in the United States in their various ways respectively. Except Chung-pa Han who is endeavoring to search for the Emersonian American dream: an ideal, a mental utopia, a place of regeneration, a glorious version of enchantment and romance, a spiritual home, Younghill Kang depicts another type of Korean exiles who are attempting to pursue their Franklinian American dream in the host land: the integrity of the family, the healthiness of competition in the society, the need for success and acquirement of material possessions. Although they attempt to realize their different American dreams of material utopia, most of these Korean immigrants are doomed to fulfill it at last.

Younghill Kang deconstructs the integrity of family in Franklinian American dream by showing Pak's dilemma of being never able to accumulate enough wealth to get back and settle down in his native land. Almost all the typical Korean exiles long for the integrity of the family in their mother land although Chung-pa Han is absorbed by his desire to find his place in American society and would have ignored, if he could have, his Korean past, his Korean identity, and his Korean compatriots. These drifting Korean exiles often give their life's savings to support the independence movement in their native land across the Pacific Ocean. Intense desire for Korean independence from Japanese occupation characterized every class of Korean living in Hawaii and the U.S. mainland for four decades. Farmers, waiters, and domestic servants by day become independence workers at night. Younghill Kang depicts Mr. Pak as one of these most typical Koreans who have the revolutionary fervor for the independence of Korea and plan to return one day to a liberated homeland:

> "He was most typical Korean, an exile only in body, not in soul. Western civilization had rolled over him as water over a rock. He was a very strong nationalist; so he always sat in at the Korean Christian services, because they had sometimes to do with nationalism. With his hard-earned money, he supported all societies for Korean revolution against Japan. Most of his relations had moved out of Korea since the Japanese occupation — into Manchuria and Russia — but Pak still lived believing that the time must come to go back… he had bought a minute piece of land to the north of Seoul. For fifteen years his single ambition had been to get back there and settle down. On Korean land, he wanted to raise 100 percent Korean children, who just be just as patriotic as himself, and maybe better educated in the classics." (Kang, 1937)[58]

According to the above vivid description, it is readily to discern that Mr. Pak wanders in the American continent only in body, not in soul and he hopes that he could have enough money to travel back, get married, settle comfortably down and bring up pure Korean descendants who are as fiercely loyal as their father. However, in the land of material utopia, the marginal ethnic group is hard to accumulate their wealth as those white people because of racial discrimination. As a houseboy who is always unemployed, Mr. Pak could never save enough money to go home for fifteen years. Thus, Younghill Kang deconstructs the integrity of family in Franklinian American dream by showing Mr. Pak's plight of being unable to scrape up enough property to return and settle down in his native land eternally.

Besides deconstructing the integrity of family of Franklinian American dream, Younghill Kang deconstructs the need for success, another aspect of material American dream, through the character of George Jum who gives up his Hollywood dream, withdraws from New York to Hawaii in seclusion and admits in frustration that he has not failed and he has only not succeeded. Since he wants to know and melt into the U.S., and since most fellow Koreans make him uncomfortable with their simple nationalism, Chung-pa Han befriends the only two exiles who are at all interested in Western literature and culture and seem successful figures in the circle of Korean exiles. George Jum, an unemployed cook who imagines himself a dapper New Yorker is the boyfriend of a white call girl. Having known Korean nobles and court officials working as waiters and houseboys in the U.S., George Jum has declined Korean culture as useless to material and psychological survival in the modern world. When he discusses Confucius with Chung-pa Han, George Jum shows his opinion:

> "Confucius, I admit, has nothing to each on the subject of love. That's where I leave him behind. For love is the beginning of a real, new and true life leading you into the Garden of Paradise, maybe Eden. It's a pity that they in English say falling in love. It is not a falling, but it is a rising. If it is a falling action, you will have no more life. But because it is a rising action, you get more done. But maybe in English they have a more ironic attitude toward love than I have…" (Kang, 1937)[41-42]

According to his statement about love, readers readily comprehend that George Jum has rejected Korean culture and accepted western ideology. In his friend's view, George Jum belongs to America because he can flirt, neck, drink and tell dirty jokes like an American college boy. Wherever he arrives, there was a chair waiting for him and a jocund audience. Unfortunately, George Jum's American dream shatters when his girlfriend finally casts him aside, which forces him to face the fact that he might be only a guest in the house of the host land. He marries a Korean American and settles down in Hawaii. Chung-pa Han receives a letter from him saying,

> "You will want to ask me about Hollywood. Only minor parts there. I was disgusted. So I have come to Hawaii… It is a hot country, and that means there is more love. I am going to get married and settle down. I am engaged to a Korean girl, one American-born, with a good stenographic training, and very pretty to see… So here in Hawaii I will spend all my hours in eating, loving and sleeping. Is love the be-all and the end-all, am I still romanticist? I never go back on my words. But what is the difference?... P.S. For the rest, I have not failed. I have only not succeeded." (Kang, 1937)[399]

According to the letter from George Jum to Chung-pa Han, readers comprehend that George Jum's American dream of the need for success at last shatters although he wants so desperately to succeed. With George Jum's abandoning his Hollywood dream, retreating from furious New York to remote Hawaii and admitting in frustration that he has not failed and he has only not succeeded, Younghill Kang deconstructs the need for success of Franklinian American dream.

With To Wan Kim who failed to assimilate into the host land as a racialized other, Younghill Kang deconstructs the third aspect of Franklinian American dream — the quest for freedom and equality, namely melting into the American society. Besides pursuing American dreams of the integrity of family and the need for success, most of Korean immigrants' quest for freedom and equality, namely melting into the American society as other Caucasians. Chung-pa Han's another friend is To Wan Kim, who has lived in the West for 16 years, supported by money sent him by his wealthy landowning parents in Korea. To Wan Kim has benefited from everything Asia had to offer: his family has a large amount of property; he is well educated in Chinese poetry; his manner is princely; he is aristocratic and cosmopolitan.

> "What tales he had to tell, and what a variety of people and scenes he remembered! In the Far East, he had wandered through the heart of storms, amidst guns and fires, battles and revolutions. He had lived long in Europe, he had visited in the Near East, even in Africa… one moment drinking the famous beer of Heidelberg, the next eating fetticini at Alfredo's in Rome, sauntering by the bookstalls in Paris, Shanghai, Tokyo, and now recalling everything over a glass of American gin in New York City." (Kang, 1937)[458]

Undoubtedly, To Wan Kim, a cosmopolitan Korean immigrant, should readily realize his American dream and melt into the U.S., a cosmopolitan country. It turns out, however, that To Wan Kim's American dream has been no more successful than George Jum's or Chung-pa Han's. To Wan Kim could claim to belong to the same brotherhood as his hero T.S. Eliot who was born in the U.S. and naturalized as a

British subject, but his rootlessness and racial alienation restrains him from being accepted by the western literary establishment as nothing more than an adopted child. As a result, his identity is always an observer, a taster, and a wanderer, never a participant. Left marooned and impecunious on a student passport when the family of the New England girlfriend he loves divides them and his own family in Korea loses their property, To Wan Kim killed himself. To Wan Kim's death is caused by rejection from his own country and alienation from the country to which he wanted so desperately to belong to. The dream of assimilation into the host land as other Caucasian immigrants from Europe is doomed to be fractured because To Wan Kim is Korean immigrant — the racialized Other who is prevented from questing for the freedom and equality.

In conclusion, instead of taking readers on an immigrant's journey from an impecunious immigrant to a successful American citizen, Younghill Kang deconstructs the mottos of progress, equality, assimilation and upward mobility advocated by American dream by his four major Korean immigrants who fail to achieve their American dreams. Though Mr. Pak is a patriot, he has to work only as a docile servant in a house and fails to go back to his colonized native land. His dream of returning home is completely smashed by the cruel reality of trapping in the U.S. George Jum tries to pretend to be American in every aspect of his life, but he is still unable to succeed melting into the host land. To Wan Kim, as a cosmopolitan Korean immigrant, is only accepted as an adopted child by the western literary establishment because of his rootlessness and racial alienation. Chung-pa Han, the narrator, also fails to integrate into American life by scholarship and study as well as an association with an American woman. By exposing the tragedies of Mr. Pak, Chung-pa Han, George Jum, and To Wan Kim, Younghill Kang demonstrates

American racial discrimination against the marginal Asian immigrants who want to find material utopia and mental utopia in the host country. Younghill Kang's *East Goes West* provides readers throughout the world with a special view of the American life from the angle of racialized other in the way of exposing a microcosm of Korean exiles in the 1920s and 1930s.

By deconstructing the two American dreams through the characters, Younghill Kang exposes that both a material Utopia and a moral Utopia are daydreams for the marginal Korean immigrants. The process of pursuing material value and spiritual harbor gradually evolves a grievous nightmare. They want to be a part of the U.S., yet they are apart by the very U.S. that advocates the notions in the unity of the family, the healthiness of competition in society, the need for success and money on a low level and emphasizes, on a high level, that the new self should be a moral self, with its duty of always becoming, always extending and newly uttering the possibilities of life. The colored people should have the self-knowledge that these glaring American dreams are not for them because they are in a de-privileging position.

Different from their contemporary writers, Sui Sin Far and Younghill Kang did not follow the routine way to satisfy the desire of the American mainstream readers. The two unique precursors banded together to delineate the first stories about the immigrant life in the host land and counterattack the accepted thinking modes. The former deconstructs the state-sanctioned thinking mode of exclusive discrimination and the latter deconstruct the American dreams. The uncommon voices from the female writer and male writer in the two branches of Northeast Asian American ethnic group outline strikingly new images of Asian Americans. Their writings are not only an act of self-assertion but an act of defiance against the weight of historical and social injunctions. The two parallel writers transcend the majority of their contemporaries and enrich our understanding of human experience. Both of them constitute a portion of the essence of the Chinese and Korean American literatures, never a mere decoration.

Unlike her peers, as the first person of Chinese descent in the United States to write and publish work about Chinese-American life, Sui Sin Far produces the first stories about Chinese American life, records their ethnic experience on the new land and draws an original and realistic picture for them in her *Mrs. Spring Fragrance and Other Writings*. Different from the most Chinese American writers in her period, she has no intention of appealing to the curiosity of the American reading public, acting as an ambassador of goodwill, and manifesting of nostalgia, reminiscence, Americanization and assimilability. She attempts to deconstruct the binary opposition in race, subvert the state-sanctioned stereotypes of Chinese people, and expose racial discrimination jeopardy so as to construct a utopian world where people of all races live harmoniously with the idea of universality of human nature as its core and one family as its form. She forces American nationals to observe and consider the world of Chinese immigrants in a fresh way so as to change these immigrants' state of being in exotic places.

In order to deconstruct the exclusive discrimination and eliminate racial binary oppositions, Sui Sin Far, from the humanity perspective, attracts the white readers to subvert their traditional prejudice against Chinese immigrants and concern the harmful result caused by the ethnocentrism and earns their sympathy and comprehension by focusing on the Chinese immigrants' physical and psychological injuries caused by the White superiority ideology, and exposing the unjust immigrant restrictions, discriminative laws and bureaucracy in "In the Land of the Free", one story of her *Mrs. Spring Fragrance*, which delineates the struggle of a Chinese immigrant couple to retrieve their son from the American government. Sui Sin Far nails penetratingly that Chinese immigrants could expect severe discrimination in a society that professes freedom and equality for all. The disastrous consequences of institutionalized racism force the white readers to realize that racial discrimination wreaked havoc on the humanity and then query the validity of *the Chinese Exclusion Act*. Thus, Sui Sin Far's stories conduce to awakening feelings of retrospection, empathy and sympathy in the White readers so that the consciousness of binary opposition of race could be deconstructed, to some extent.

Deconstruction of the binary opposition in race and exposure of racial discrimination jeopardization are not Sui Sin Far's ultimate goal because she wants to construct a utopian world. Against the oriental view of the East as the inferior Other and the West superiority, Sui Sin Far challenged the cultural hegemony of Western colonial discourse by explaining the reality and exposing universality of human nature in a Chinese couple and an interracial couple respectively in both *In the Land of the Free* and *The Story of One White Woman Who Married a Chinese*. Holding the view of "the whole world as one family" with the idea of universality of human nature as its core and one family as its form, Sui Sin Far attempts to reconstruct a utopian community by depicting the humanity of Chinese Americans and promoting ethnic integration and harmony between White Americans and Chinese Americans. Focusing on the universality of human nature in the Chinese Americans and Chinese immigrants, Sui Sin Far subverts and deconstructs the stereotypes of Chinese people in American mainstream society. Thus, a utopian world with the idea of universality of human nature as its core and one family as its form was reconstructed by the emphasis on the equality of human nature and deconstruction of the racist nature. As a complex and insightful treatment of Asian identity and the Asian immigrant experience, *Mrs. Spring Fragrance* deconstructs racial stereotypes and displays the absolute difference between imaginary characters in Orientalism and the real Chinese immigrants so as to query the western cultural hegemony.

As the only and first Korean immigrant to write novels in English in the first-generation Korean American writers by 1965, Younghill Kang describes his experiences in the U.S., which is different from most Korean immigrant writers of the first generation in his period who focused on the Korean patriotic spirit and memories of Korea instead of Korean Americans in the U.S. in their literature. Instead of taking readers on an immigrant's journey from a penniless immigrant to a successful citizen, Younghill Kang deconstructs the mottos of progress, equality, assimilation and upward mobility advocated by the U.S. with his four major Korean immigrants who fail to achieve their American dreams in *East Goes West*. By intersecting Emersonian American dream and Franklinian American dream through the characters, Younghill Kang reveals that both a material Utopia and a moral Utopia are daydreams for the marginal Korean immigrants. Their process of pursuing material value and spiritual harbor gradually evolves a heartbreaking nightmare. They want to be a part of the U.S., yet they are apart by the very U.S. that advocates beliefs in the unity of the family, the healthiness of competition in society, the need for success and money on a low level and emphasizes that the new self should be a moral self, with its duty of always becoming, always extending and newly uttering the possibilities of life on a high level.

With the portrayal of the sundry male characters in *East Goes West*, Younghill Kang intertwined and deconstructed two kinds of American dreams, respectively.

East Goes West is the miserable record of Chung-pa Han's unsuccessful search for his Emersonian American dream of his imagination — a mental utopia which is a place of regeneration, a glorious version of fascination and romance, and a secular format of a spiritual home. At the very beginning of the novel, Younghill Kang constructs his protagonist's Emersonian American dream — seeking an opening into American life through scholarship and study in order to seek out a secular format of a mental utopia. Then Younghill Kang deconstructs Chung-pa Han's Emersonian American dream by his failure to quest it. In the process of pursuing his mental utopia, Chung-pa Han is exploited, ridiculed, despised, mistreated, and utilized by various employers and whites. Chung-pa Han's failure to fulfill his dream comes from his experiences at the margins of the U.S. though he constructs his spiritual utopia through the mainstream western classics. Chung-pa Han finds out the secret core of the world in his dream — hypocrisy, covetousness and desperation without enchantment and romance he expected before. Thus, Chung-pa Han's Emersonian American dream dies through his picaresque adventures which expose the shallow materialism, hypocrisy, philistinism and inhumanity of life in capitalist America. With Chung-pa Han's failure to find an entry into American life, contradictions between the promise of freedom and the reality of racial discrimination, between economic survival and dreams of intellectual accomplishment, and between the ideal of America and actual experience of life in its margins still remain although Chung-pa Han clings to his naive faith in America's shining promise.

Younghill Kang deconstructs the unity of the family, the need for success, the quest for freedom and equality and acquirement of material possessions advocated by Franklinian American dream by his four major Korean immigrants who fail to achieve their American dreams: Mr. Pak, the nationalist, is marooned in the U.S., working as a domestic houseboy and failing to achieve the dream of returning to his colonized homeland; George Jum, the gadfly, tries to be American in his all walks of his life, in the end, admits that he has not failed and he has only not succeeded; To Wan Kim, the aristocrat, fails to gain access to American high culture and commits suicide finally; Chung-pa Han, the narrator, finds no entry into American life by both reading Shakespeare and befriending an American woman. Through drifting adventures of Mr. Pak, Chung-pa Han, George Jum, and To Wan Kim, Younghill Kang demonstrates the view of the unfair and illogic of American racial discrimination against Asian immigrants which makes the immigrants' American dreams doom to fail. *East Goes West* presents an objective view of the American life from the perspectives of people banned by the racial discrimination and reveals moments in the lives of the invisible ethnic group to American readers — Korean exiles in the 1920s and 1930s.

Harboring and adoring the American dream which stands for the promising future and the new start, the Korean exiled intellectuals soon realize, however, that there is a discrepancy between the west he knows from literature and the west he experiences. Through the dramatized conflicts, the major characters fail to achieve their American dreams: the integrity of the family, the healthiness of competition in the society, the need for success and acquirement of material possessions and assimilation into a place of regeneration, a glorious version of enchantment and romance, and a secular format of a spiritual home, for these glaring American dreams are not for the colored marginal people in a de-privileging position.

Chapter 4

Conclusion

The rapid development of Chinese and Korean American literatures in the Anglo world has attracted the attention of the world. Their double-voiced discourses not only wrestle with contradiction between their native cultures and the host culture but also subvert and transcend the conventional euro-centric tradition. Their rise in America and their popularity around the world are a challenge to the modern western dichotomous world-view, or master/slave metaphor. From the very beginning, both Chinese and Korean immigrant writers have been engaged in the struggle with racial discrimination in that, historically, Chinese and Korean Americans were materially and discursively excluded from the mainstream of American life, denied subjectivity and defined instead according to the degree of threat they were thought to pose to the dominant culture at the particular points in time.

Chinese and Korean American writings emerge from the context of a century and a half of persistent and deeply rooted racist inscriptions of Asians in both official and mass culture as grotesquely alien others. Pressed to demonstrate the falseness of these representations, the Chinese and Korean American writers of the first generation often attempt to present the true story. They articulate double-voiced discourses to demonstrate what they really are. The most works by Chinese American writers of the first generation display such multiple characteristics as self-appointed ambassadors of goodwill, acculturation, protest against racial discrimination and appeal for acceptance and tolerance in the new land, reformatory and activist's view about how literature could serve political ends, sad wails, the cultural transformation of Chinese American literature in the new land based on the emigrant experiences, and the plantation life, generational conflict and local affairs in Hawaii. Different from multiplicity of most Chinese American writings, most of Korean American writers grapple in different ways with the effects of Japanese colonization on Koreans and Korean Americans. Only now, more than half a century after the Second World War has this concern begun to become muted in Korean American writings, which can be expected to address an ever-increasing array of other themes. Although the highly diverse individual voices of Chinese American writers and Korean American writers are reducible to no single measure, their recurrent themes and techniques reflect psychological and cultural dilemmas specific to Chinese Americans and Korean Americans. These writers spiritually witness routine social brutality, tell stories about and for those previously left out of the literary and social text, make claims for the powerless, and reveal the courage and resourcefulness of people generally believed to be invisible and inarticulate.

The multiplicity in Chinese American literature and nationalism in Korean American literature derived the unbalanced number of works and the points of view in literary expression. It is no wonder that there was the relatively small number of published Korean American writings in English compared with that by Chinese immigrants and Chinese Americans in this period because there always has been a larger proportion of English-speaking Chinese American writers than Korean

American writers in the early stage. Different arrival times shaped the layers and communities of Asian Americans. Moreover, both international and American circumstances change with alteration inside the two countries of China and Korea in different time periods. Thus, the number of writings and multiple points of view vary in Chinese American literature and Korean American literature in their own early stages.

As are previously studied, despite differences existing between Chinese and Korean American literatures, some main commonalities between them could be discerned. First, like Chinese American literature, members of an elite class of educated immigrants uttered the early voice of Korean American literature largely in the form of autobiography. The minority represent the majority in two branches of ethnic American literature. Then, the body of Chinese American literature and Korean American literature shares the similar literature thematic concerns such as love, desire for personal freedom and acceptance by the American mainstream society, struggles against oppression and injustice, and expression of the immigrants' desire to find a place for themselves in American life and culture. Furthermore, books by Chinese and Koreans in the United States recollecting their Asian childhoods have found many readers in the West. Lee Yan Phou's *When I Was a Boy in China* (1887) was the first of these, while New Il-han's *When I Was a Boy in Korea* (1928) was one of the last. Moreover, both Chinese and Korean immigrant workers vanished without leaving behind much written account of their individual immigrant experiences in America with the exception of *Island: Poetry and History of Chinese Immigrants on Angel Island, 1910–1940*. Chinese and Korean migrants had the similar migration experience. Thousands of Chinese and Koreans migrated to the United States and Hawaii, which was prompted by active recruitment of labor for plantations, railroads, mining and field work. The relatively small Chinese and Korean population consisted largely of laborers who had no means or inclination to return to their homelands. Their points of view on the immigrant experiences were rarely presented in writings in English or even in their own mother tongues. However, some unknown immigrants carved poems in Chinese into the walls of the barracks on Angel Island, where they were held before being permitted to enter the United States between 1910 and 1940. Him Mark Lai, Genny Lim, and Judy Yung translated and preserved the Chinese immigrant voice in American history and culture in *Island: Poetry and History of Chinese Immigrants on Angel Island, 1910–1940,* which was published in 1980. The rare presentation of early immigrant experiences is partly because the general privation and loneliness of immigrant life repressed the desire to represent, partly because their time was consumed in struggles for a livelihood, partly because Chinese and Korean writers could hardly know where to begin and what readers to address in the face of pervasive American ignorance of and antipathy towards Asians, and partly because many early Chinese and Korean immigrants neither learned English nor realized the culture as something that belonged to them as they were segregated from the mainstream of American social and economic life and prevented by law from becoming naturalized American citizens with voting and civil rights. In addition, in China and Korea, writing and literature were the domain of the literati who traditionally majored in poetry and classical essays. Autobiography and popular fiction were not in the tradition of Chinese and Korean cultures in that autobiographical writing was virtually unknown, since for a scholar to write a book about himself would have been viewed egotistical in the extreme, and fiction was considered frivolous. As a result, the early Chinese and Korean immigrants rarely record their points of view on the immigrant experiences. Fifth, in order to counterattack the false representation of alien others, early Korean immigrants and Chinese American writers often tried to present the true story by displaying how Asian immigrants could become successfully westernized or Americanized because Korean immigrants and Korean Americans, like Chinese immigrants and Chinese Americans, were excluded from the mainstream of American society and defined differently by the degree of the threat they were thought to pose to the dominance in the different periods of time throughout the history. Sixth, they are both shaped by vital particulars in the U.S. and Asian orientation. For example, American racism is a vital factor in the Chinese and Korean experiences in the U.S. Hence it is no wonder that literatures by both Chinese American and Korean American writers are often concerned with this shared heritage. Racial policies and attitudes towards the Chinese and Korean groups are quite similar, so they have the similar responses to these policies and attitudes. Thus, the reactions to the racial discrimination have the same emotional resonance in literature written by the first generation of immigrants from China and Korea. Last, uprooted from the old native world which is still one indispensable and interconnected part of their being, both the Chinese immigrant writers and Korean immigrant writers tend to express the experience of uprootedness and all its attendant sense of loss, sadness, nostalgia and disillusionment. Meanwhile, they adopt the role of spokesmen by virtue of their achievements. To mediate between the old and the new worlds or between the ghetto and the American society, they prefer the former to the latter. Given the ignominious history of the greater racial and cultural barriers that Chinese immigrants and Korean immigrants experienced, the early-stage Chinese American writers and Korean American writers used the spokesperson's role to a much greater extent.

Generally speaking, due to the ethnic writers' internal duality, both Chinese American literature and Korean American literature as two branches of American ethnic literature fulfill the high seriousness of literature as a criticism of history and life.

Different from their contemporary writers who have the intention of appealing to the curiosity of the American reading public, acting as an ambassador of goodwill, and manifesting of nostalgia, reminiscence, Americanization and assimilability, or mainly focus on the Korean memory, both Sui Sin Far and Younghill Kang are unique in their literary circles, to some extent. As precursors in the Chinese and Korean American literatures, they subvert the ideal America by deconstructing of the state-sanctioned thinking mode of exclusive discrimination and the mottos of progress, equality, assimilation and upward mobility advocated by American dreams in their works from different perspectives as a woman and a man, respectively. They restore and record the struggling life of our immigrant ancestors on the new land through writing about an almost-forgotten past.

In *Mrs. Spring Fragrance*, Sui Sin Far offers alternative perspectives on the immigrant life of the first-generation Chinese Americans and actively challenges mainstream readers' preconceptions. She deconstructs the thinking mode of exclusive discrimination based on racial binary oppositions, ethnocentrism and scientific racialism by subverting the state-sanctioned racial stereotyped Other and exposing racial discrimination jeopardy so as to construct a utopian world where people of all races live harmoniously with the idea of universality of human nature as its core and one family as its form. By doing so, she speaks on behalf of the Other who has been silenced at the margin, and dramatizes the injustices that plagues race relations in the U.S.

Against the strategy within the early Korean American literature by most first-generation Korean American writers to define resistance in oppositional terms to Japanese or Western imperial culture, Younghill Kang turns his attention away from the anti-Japanese nationalism of many of his contemporaries, attempting instead to challenge the imagining of a pure, monolithic white hegemonic U.S. culture. Rather than look back as did many of his similarly displaced fellow Koreans, Younghill Kang deconstructs the mottos of progress, equality, assimilation and upward mobility advocated by the U.S. with his four major Korean immigrants who fail to achieve their American dreams in *East Goes West*. By intersecting Emersonian American dream and Franklinian American dream through the characters, Younghill Kang reveals that both a material Utopia and a moral Utopia are daydreams for the marginal Korean immigrants. Their process of pursuing material value and spiritual harbor gradually evolves a heartbreaking nightmare. They want to be a part of the U.S., yet they are apart by the very U.S. that advocates beliefs in the unity of the family, the healthiness of competition in society, the need for success and money on a low level and emphasizes that the new self should be a moral self, with its duty of always becoming, always extending and newly uttering the possibilities of life on a high level.

When the names of Sui Sin Far, Younghill Kang and other Chinese American and Korean American writers are mentioned more frequently by readers and literary critics, those pioneering writers who have sown the seed before them should not be forgotten. It is in the recorded usable past by these predecessors that the Chinese American and Korean American cultural heritages are passed from one generation to another. These pages nurtured successors with inspiration and help people see more clearly the progress of Chinese Americans and Korean Americans and their communities and changes taken place within the groups since the very beginning. It is worth reconsidering the importance and impact of the early writings when Chinese American literature and Korean American literature are entering a new era and facing a diversifying future. It is clear that our cultural warriors capture the living experience of Asian American people, to the everlasting benefit of our future generations. The double-voiced discourses of the first-generation immigrant writers echo each other and build bridges that span generations and nationalities between men and women, connecting Asian Americans to each other, to other minority groups, to American society and beyond. Thus, the hegemony of racist writing about Asians and Asian Americans is being challenged each time Chinese and Korean American voices emerge in an effort to define and express the unique and ever-evolving Asian American experience.

By the analysis of early Chinese American literature and Korean American literature, the commonalities and differences could be detected within the context of a shared American experience and Northeast Asian origin, and meanwhile reflect the variety, diversity, and indeed the unevenness of the two branches in ethnic American literature. Through this book, the author hopes to present an alternative view and thus broaden the study of Asian American literature.

As one part of Asian American literature, both Chinese and Korean American literatures are our voices to the rest of the world. Our diversity and uniqueness can and should be boosted rather than misused as a justification for inequality and inferiority. They demonstrate our humanity and our interconnections and help us define our identity, culture, community, our unity and our diversity. As such they have the potential to contribute to our sovereignty and the preservation of our cultural integrity, far from splitting Asian Americans from the rest of American society. The cross-national comparison could enable us to identify the particular experiences of each group, to highlight the common experiences of both of us, and to inspect ourselves, China and Korea more objectively. In some future, perhaps we will all enjoy without limitation being equal though not alike.

Bibliography

AMMONS E, 1991. Conflicting stores: American women writers at the turn into the twentieth century[M]. New York: Oxford University Press.

ANDERSON M L, TAYLOR H F, 2006. Sociology: understanding a diverse society[M]. Belmont: Wadsworth Publishing Company.

BERNER H, 2003. Home is where the heart is? identity and belonging in Asian American literature[D]. Bochum: Ruhr-Universität Bochum.

BERRY C J, 2006. Aristotle, Hobbes and Chimpanzees[J]. Political studies, 54 (4): 827–845.

BIGGERS E D, 1925. The house without a key[M]. New York: Collier.

BRENNAN T, 1990. The national longing for form[M]//BHABHA H. Nation and narration. New York: Routledge.

CHEUNG K, 1993. Articulate silences: Hisaye Yamanoto, Maxine Hong Kinston, Joy Kogawa [M]. Ithaca: Cornell University Press.

CHEUNG K, 1997. Re-viewing Asian American literary studies[M]//CHEUNG K. An interethnic companion to Asian American literature. Cambridge: Cambridge University Press.

CHIN F, 1972. Confessions of the Chinatown cowboy[J]. Bulletin of Asian scholars (4): 58–70.

CHIN F, CHAN J P, FUSADINADA L, et al., 1974. Aiiieeeee!: An anthology of

Asian American writers[M]. Washington D.C.: Howard University Press.

CH'OE Y, 1989. Korean literature in America[J]. Modern praxis (9): 59–66.

CHOI S N, 1993. Echoes of the white giraffe[M]. Boston: Houghton Mifflin Harcourt.

EATON E, 1995. Leaves from the mental portfolio of a Eurasian[M]//LING A, WHITE-PARKS A. Mrs. Spring Fragrance and other writings. Urbana: University of Illinois Press.

FANON F, 1968. The wretched of the earth[M]. New York: Grove Press.

FERENS D, 2002. Edith and Winnifred Eaton: Chinatown missions and Japanese romances[M]. Chicago: University of Illinois Press.

FUSE M P, 2001. Richard E. Kim[M]//HUANG G. Asian American autobiographers: a bio-bibliographical critical sourcebook. Westport, Conn.: Greenwood Publishing Group.

GRASTON H P, 1916. As a Chinaman saw us[M]//GRASTON H P. Asian commentary on America. New York: D. Appleton & Co.

GUAN H, 2007. Seeking identity between worlds: a study of Chinese American women's literature[M]. Kaifeng: Henan University Press.

HAN J, 1996. Korean-American literature[M]//KNIPPLING A S. New immigrant literatures in the United States: a sourcebook to our multicultural literary heritage. Westport, Conn.: Greenwood Publishing Group.

HOLFORD D V, 2001. Biracial/bicultural identity in the writings of Sui Sin Far[J]. MELUS, 26 (2): 159–186.

HONG K, 2002. Chaemi Hanguk imin chakkadsos chakpum yngu[J]. Huangungma lkrhak (17): 1–36.

HSU H L, 2011. Mrs. Spring Fragrance[M]. Peterborough: Broadview Press.

KANG Y, 1931. The grass roof[M]. New York: Charles Scribner's Sons.

KANG Y, 1937. East goes west[M]. New York: Charles Scribner's Sons.

KIM E H, 1990. "Such opposite creatures": men and women in Asian American literature[J]. Michigan quarterly review, 29 (1): 68–93.

KIM E H, 1997. Korean American literature[M]//CHEUNG K. An interethnic companion to Asian American literature. Cambridge: Cambridge University Press.

KIM E H, 2004. Roots and wings: an overview of Korean American literature 1934–2003[C]//YOUNG-KEY K, GRINKER R R, LARSEN K W. Korean American literature. Washington D.C.: The George Washington University.

KIM E H, 2006. Asian American literature: an introduction to the writings and their social context[M]. Beijing: Foreign Language Teaching and Research Press.

KOSTELANETZ R, 1972. Seeing through shunk[M]//FRANK C, CHAN J P. Racist love. New York: Ballantine Books.

KUNITZ S, 1955. Twentieth century authors[M]. New York: H. W. Wilson.

LAI H M, LIM G, YUNG J, 1991. Island: poetry and history of Chinese immigrants on Angel Island, 1910–1940[M]. Seattle: University of Washington Press.

LING A, 1990. Between worlds: women writers of Chinese ancestry[M]. New York: Pergamon Press.

LING A, WHITE-PARKS A, 1995. Introduction to Mrs. Spring Fragrance and other writings[M]//SUI S F. Mrs. Spring Fragrance and other writings. Urbana: University of Illinois Press.

LOWE L, 1991. Heterogeneity, hybridity, multiplicity: Asian American difference[J]. Diaspora: a journal of transnational studies (1): 24–44.

LOWE L, 1996. Immigrant acts: on Asian American cultural politics[M]. Durham: Duke University Press.

LOW V, 1982. The unimpressible race: a century of educational struggle by the Chinese in San Francisco[M]. New Delhi: East/West Pub. Co.

MADISON J, 1788. The structure of the government must furnish the proper checks and balances between the different departments[J]. Independent journal (2) [2021–09–18]. https://www.gutenberg.org/cache/epub/1404/pg1404-images.html#link2H_4_0051.

MARGOLIS D R, 1998. The fabric of self[M]. New Haven: Yale University Press.

MERTON R K, 1996. On social structure and science[M]. Chicago: University of Chicago Press.

MOON H J, 1976. The Korean immigrants in America: the quest of identity in the formative years, 1903–1918[D]. Reno: University of Nevada, Reno.

MOORE-GILBERT B, 1997. Postcolonial theory: contexts, practices, politics[M]. London: Verso.

MULLEN B, LINKON S, 1996. Radical revisions: rereading 1930s culture[M]. Urbana: University of Illinois Press.

OH S, 2007. The martyred[M]. Encyclopedia of American Asian-American literature. New York: Facts on File.

PATTERSON W K, 1977. The Korean frontier in America: immigration to Hawaii, 1896–1910[D] Philadelphia: University of Pennsylvania.

POOLE R, 1999. Nation and identity[M]. New York: Routledge.

SAID E, 1979. Orientalism[M]. New York: Vintage.

SAID E, 1995. Orientalism, an afterword[J]. Raritan (14): 32–59.

STRONGMAN K T, 1996. The psychology of emotion: theories of emotion in perspective[M]. Chichester: John Wiley&Sons.

SUDESH M, 2002. Diaspora criticism[M]. Edinburgh: Edinburgh University Press.

SUI S F, 1995. Mrs. Spring Fragrance and other writings[M]. Urbana: University of Illinois Press.

TAKAKI R, 1989. Strangers from a different shore: a history of Asian Americans [M]. New York: Little, Brown and Company.

TYSON L, 1999. Critical theory today: a user-friendly guide[M]. New York: Garland Publishing Inc.

TSIANG H T, 1931. China red[M]. New York: The Liberal Press, Inc.

WHITE-PARKS A, 1995. Sui Sin Far/Edith Maude Eaton: a literary biography[M]. Chicago: University of Illinois Press.

WONG S C, 1993. Reading Asian American literature: from necessity to extravagance [M]. Princeton, New Jersey: Princeton University Press.

WONG S C, 1997. Chinese American literature[M]//CHEUNG K. An interethnic companion to Asian American literature. New York: Cambridge University Press.

WU W F, 1982. The yellow peril: Chinese Americans in American fiction, 1850–1940 [M]. Hamden, Conn.: Archon Books.

WU T, 2002. America through the spectacles of an oriental diplomat[M]. Taiyuan: Shanxi Education Press.

YIM L, 1951. My forty year fight for Korea[M]. New York: American Book-Stratford Press.

YIN Xiaohuang, 2000. Chinese American literature since the1850s[M]. Urbana: University of Illinois Press.

ZO K Y, 1971. Chinese emigration into the United States, 1850–1880[M]. Ann Arbor, Mich.: University Microfilms International.

陈依范，1985. 美国华人[M]. 郁怡民，郁苓，译. 北京：工人出版社.

容闳，2003. 容闳自传：我在美国和中国的生活[M]. 石霓，译注. 上海：百家出版社.

赵一凡，张中载，李德恩，2006. 西方文论关键词[M]. 北京：外语教学与研究出版社.

http://www.academia.edu/525535/Covert_Language_Ideologies_in_Korean_American_Literature_unpublished_#.